MW01241005

Copyright © 2020 by Shaun Hutson & Matt Shaw

ISBN: 978-1-71696-707-8

Matt Shaw Publications

All rights reserved. This book or any portion thereof

may not be reproduced or used in any manner whatso-

ever

without the express written permission of the publisher

except for the use of brief quotations in a book review.

The characters in this book are purely fictitious.

Any likeness to persons living or dead is purely coinci-

dental.

www.facebook.com/mattshawpublications

Matt Shaw

Signed Books and more
www.mattshawpublications.co.uk

Shaun Hutson

www.shaunhutson.com

How The Book Came To Be:

It was a strange day. I was sitting there, minding my own business, when suddenly an email pinged through to my inbox:

Hello Matt,

I hope you're well in this fucking madness and virus bullshit. This is just a quick message to see if you're okay. I'm uninfected as far as I know.
I wonder if there could a novel done with this fucking virus as a background?
Just wondering...
I know we've had "world wiped out by disease" books and films hundreds of times before but not THIS fucking virus.
Anyway, I'll send a longer message soon.
Look after yourself.
Shaun

Well that was thoroughly nice of him, I thought. Shaun and I have exchanged a number of colourful emails over the years after meeting at a convention. I've put his work in a couple of anthologies I have compiled since then, and he was good enough to throw some suggestions at me for my film script (MONSTER; available now on Amazon), but I never thought I would actually get to work with him. Not that such a thought would stop me putting the seed in his head in these troubled times...

Hi Shaun,

I've already been thinking about doing a novella for the virus. I reckon I could get it turned around pretty fast... Perfect timing with people stuck at home looking for new things to read! Hell, if you're bored and wanted to write with me - could be great working together. I've done it before where each person does a chapter before sending it back; each chapter done on a different character living through isolation.

I am well though, thanks for asking. I am surprised especially as I was in

Germany and America before this kicked off. But then, I MIGHT have had it because I had a bad cough and cold type thing in the states but, fuck knows.

Glad to hear you're well and not infected! Try and stay that way,

I'd be a tad upset if anything happened to you.

Matt

I mean, I *wanted* to work with Shaun but it was just a throw away comment if I am going to be honest. He's a busy guy and who am I? Just some cunt chancing his luck because the world was ending, Hell has frozen over (you can tell because McDonalds closed their restaurants) and we're all pretty much doomed. If he was ever going to say "yes" then *now* would be the time.

Matt,

Had you got any specific ideas about what the novella might entail? I've had a couple of ideas about a Corona Virus type thing but only with the virus as the background, the reason streets are deserted etc.
If people went missing it would be harder to discover and would take longer to uncover if the dozy fuckers were all self-isolating...

I'll try and put a synopsis or something together and you can have a look at it and see what you think. See if the two of us can come up with something quick and repulsive :)

All the best, mate,

Shaun

And that was it. From there, we were away… You know how it ends because you're holding the book now and, thank you for that.

We hope you enjoy it and it gives you a good enough reason to stay in, during these troubling times. If our book keeps you out of harm's way then, mission accomplished! One word of warning though: don't follow the lead of the characters within this book… It probably won't end well for you.

A two word horror story:

He coughed.

The Tainted

Souls

Shaun Hutson

&

Matt Shaw

"I don't believe in this world anymore."

- Seether

1

It was the end of the world.

At least that was how it appeared.

A scene from some Hollywood blockbuster that depicted the earth being ravaged by aliens or disease. Only this time, it was real. It was actually happening. It wasn't all going to come to an end when the house lights went up. This time, it was for keeps.

From the window of her second floor flat, Tessa Meyer could see the nearby underpass, the pathway that led beneath it and the road that it supported.

They were deserted.

They had been for the last week or so. If half a dozen cars a day passed over the road above the underpass it was a busy day. She'd seen people walking along the pathways next to where she lived but, during the last few days, even that meagre number had dwindled to all but nothing. There was a woman in her sixties who always walked a yappy little dog, no matter what the weather but even she had failed to show lately.

There was a family living in the house across the street who, like clockwork, every morning at 8.15, piled into the mother's 4X4 to be ferried to school and work but, for the last week, Tessa hadn't seen hide nor hair of them either. They hadn't even left the house. Many of the residents around her hadn't. Some, like herself, made the odd trip to supermarkets in search of anything that hadn't been snatched up by the morons who thought panic buying was an instruction rather than an insult.

Tessa had also decided, during her period of self-isolation or social distancing or whatever the fucking powers that be were calling it these days, that she would try and get more exercise. A walk to the local shop and back (a distance of about half a mile) would help her get active and also to breathe some fresh air although that term was somewhat redundant considering the Corona Virus was airborne. Use all the hand sanitizer you wanted, wash your mitts as often as was possible, scrub them until the skin came off, it didn't matter. The Covid-19 Virus was airborne. It moved through the air you fucking dummies. You inhaled it. Without you knowing, it infiltrated your airwaves and it took up residence in your lungs or your throat.

Tessa shuddered involuntarily as she thought of that fact and she glanced behind her towards the TV as she tired momentarily of peering out of the window.

The newsreader was droning on about how many had died of the virus, how many now had it, how many were expected to catch it. And, the punchline, how many were *expected* to die of it. Tessa sighed, crossed to the TV and switched it off. She didn't want to hear any more. Didn't *need* to. She'd long ago tired of it. Depressed by the severity of the virus and the effect it was having and the constant tone of devastation. It didn't seem to get any better. No news of a cure. No sign of anyone getting better (if there was, the news programmes didn't consider it as enthralling as the talk of more deaths and infections). Just more shops closing, more businesses going bust, more pubs being outlawed.

She returned to her vigil at the window, wiping some condensation from the glass, watching as several droplets trickled down the pane like gleaming tears.

She heard a noise outside and thought that a vehicle was actually passing along the previously deserted road but she looked more closely and saw she was mistaken.

The noise must have come from one of the other flats, she reasoned.

There were eleven others in the small block, most unoccupied due to the high rents but the one directly above her was the domain of a couple a little younger than herself.

Peter and Claire. She only knew their first names. She'd only spoken to them a couple of times when she'd taken in parcels for them and they'd come to collect them. They seemed nice enough. Quiet. He worked in London at a publishers. She worked at a local call centre. He'd been working at home for the last two weeks, she'd just been laid off. There wasn't much call for telesales of loft insulation to over sixties in the current climate. If the poor old sods were self isolating they certainly didn't want some person pretending to be a surveyor lumbering around in their loft.

Tessa sighed again and decided that the best thing to do was to venture out. She was short of milk and teabags and just hoped those hadn't been stripped from the already sparse shelves in the nearest supermarket. No doubt some idiots had been wheeling trolleys around Tesco and Morrisons filling them with goods as if they were extras on "Supermarket Sweep" rather than sufferers in the middle of the worst pandemic since 1918.

Tessa let out a breath and wandered through to her bedroom to get her coat.

Outside, it had begun to rain.

2.

The streets were near-deserted on the best of days, both on the pavements and the roads. Today was quieter than usual though with the viral threat being worse than anyone had thought. Most of the stores were closed. Some had their shutters down and others just with a notice in their window warning of "closure for the foreseeable future".

The heavy clouds hanging low in the sky beat away the grime with a constant rain and, for the first time, the city looked clean. It wouldn't stay like that. The moment the people were allowed out of their houses - out of the government forced quarantine - the dirt, filth and general pollution would return and no lessons would have been learned. For now though, the world was almost starting to look new, to some at least. To others it was eerie. *The End Of Days*; the beginning of the end. With similar situations happening in cities across the world, maybe the doomsayers were right this time? Maybe these were the End Days and the human race was living on borrowed time although, if people weren't socially distancing themselves, someone would have probably argued that mankind was on borrowed time the moment certain politicians came to power in their respective countries.

The virus, CO-VID 19, made people stop and look around at the bigger picture of the world they live in. They saw that the world was fucked but the truth of the matter was, the planet was broken long before the virus leaked its way across the globe from a shitty little market-place in Wuhan, China.

*

With the quietness of the streets, the car could be heard from a long way away. Its low-growling engine rumbling over the horizon gradually getting louder as it neared. Its lights were seen first, illuminating the path before it. Then, the car slid around the corner. The occupants laughing all the way as the driver made the most of the lack of traffic.

The car skidded momentarily as the backend escaped the control of the driver. A little opposite lock on the steering wheel brought it back under control before the car slowed to a halt. The passenger door opened and Anett Schwertner, a young German woman with bright red hair, jumped out cursing the driver in the process.

'You're an asshole.'

The driver door opened and a dark haired lad climbed out, laughing. Adam Wood. The reckless driving had been for Anett's benefit, just to scare the shit out of her.

Adam said, 'Come on, get back in the car.'

'Fuck you!'

'You're a dick,' Dave Anscheit said, as he climbed from the back of the car. He had told Adam that Anett got travel sick so there was no reason for Adam to drive like that other than to be a dick.

'Calm your tits. I was having a fuckin' laugh.'

'Yeah. Funny. Prick.' Anett turned to Dave and told him, 'I'm not getting back in the car.'

The pair had travelled over from Germany together. It was meant to be a vacation to catch up with some English friends but then, they had found themselves stuck after the closure of their borders back home.

As the trio continued arguing, Chris Whiteman climbed from the back of the car too. He didn't give a shit what the others were saying though. He just wanted to get the fuck out and stretch his legs.

Chris had been going stir-crazy back in his apartment; a feeling made worse because his partner, Anne Lambley, had left him just before the quarantine had begun. He didn't even know where she'd gone for her own lock-down. She wasn't answering his calls, she wasn't reading his texts; she simply ghosted him like the dirty cunt that she was.

'Come on,' Adam was saying, 'get back in the fucking car.'

'No!'

'I'm sorry! I was just playing around. I'll drive normal, yeah? Just for you, you fucking princess.'

'Fuck you.'

'Come on, you two…' Dave tried to play peacekeeper to little avail. He was just as desperate to get back in the car as Adam was. The local supermarket, usually twenty-four hours, was closing for the night to give the staff a chance to re-stock the shelves. With food running out at home, Dave was desperate to get to the supermarket to grab some supplies. The longer these two idiots argued, the more chance the rest of the hunter-gatherers would strip the shelves bare.

'I told you I'm not getting back in the…'

Adam cut Anett off, 'Then fucking don't. Walk back home.'

'Guys…'

Dave was also cut off by the sound of glass smashing. All three turned in the direction of the noise. Chris was standing by the broken window of a locked-up Off-Licence. They watched, surprised, as Chris casually leaned in through the broken window and pulled out a bottle of whiskey. Without a word, Chris spun the lid off the bottle and took a swig. He swallowed hard as he realised the others were watching him.

Chris held the bottle out and asked, 'Drink anyone?'

There was a slight pause before Adam laughed, with Chris following close behind. Dave and Anett were a lit-

tle more hesitant with their laughter but, it soon followed, if only to fit in with their hosts.

Dave said, 'English are fucking crazy!'

3.

It wasn't just the English that were "crazy".

All around the world, in countries struggling to contain the virus from spreading further, societies were crumbling amidst the confusion, misinformation and panic.

The good people were few and far between, with their kind offers to help those in less fortunate positions, and the idiots were seemingly out in force treating the pandemic as a joke or opportunity to fuck up someone's day.

Jump to different locations around the world:

A homeless man in Washington had been told to self-quarantine himself, after being told he had contracted the virus. With nowhere to go, he ended up walking back out into the streets, coughing his germs everywhere. What was worse was the fact that the people treating him, the ones who *knew* the severity of the situation just let him go despite how contagious he was.

Meanwhile, more and more racist attacks were happening against the Chinese, as they found themselves being blamed for what had happened to the world. Some got away with a few cuts and bruises whilst others ended up in hospital; machines around them - beeping noisily - keeping them alive; their faces staved in beyond human recognition and their loved ones sitting, anxiously, around the bedside.

A woman was arrested for going up to someone and purposely coughing in their face before telling them, 'I was ill and now you are too.'

Another couple was arrested in Italy, ignoring the *strict* quarantine measures in order to satisfy their sexual itch with a quick fuck in their car as - elsewhere still - televisions were showing News reports featuring young people not caring about what was being said about the virus as they sunned themselves on overly crowded beaches. *We paid for the trip so why shouldn't we take it?*

Then of course you had the mindless pricks who did do the right thing by staying in their home but still fucked things up for people by spending their days posting inaccurate "scare" facts to their social media accounts, which caused their friends to panic as no one knew what to truly believe anymore. It was these idiots which caused the mass-rush to buy all stock of toilet paper...

The looting hadn't started yet, no doubt thanks to the way entire cities were being locked down or because there was nothing left to steal from the supermarkets. With tempers on the rise though, it was only ever going to be a matter of time before the crowds gathered and the violence escalated further.

The virus had only been made aware to the public within the last couple of months.

This was only the beginning and all government bodies across the world were warning the same thing: it is going to get worse.

Dave said, 'English are fucking crazy!'

4.

Dave adjusted the glasses on his nose, pushing them up further to the bridge. This was a topic of conversation he could get behind: *what caused the virus.*

'There are people,' he said, interrupting Adam's re-counting of a news article he had seen which blamed the virus on the "eating of bats", 'who believe it is a bioweapon released upon the world.'

Anett rolled her eyes from the front of the car, now that they were back on the road to the store. She had heard all of Dave's theories back in Germany, before they left for England. Every day it was something new and, every day it was something he believed to be true. When Anett would ask him about the previous theory he had, Dave would shrug it off as though he had never mentioned it in the first place.

'A bioweapon which has impacted the whole world. That's fucking dumb,' Adam said as Chris took another swig from the stolen liquor. 'Who the fuck would release something that fucks *everyone* up. In war, there is usually a winner, you know?'

Dave leaned forward so that his face poked between the front two seats of the car. 'Well,' Dave said, 'you think there is no clear winner but there is.'

Adam didn't take his eyes from the road. 'Yeah? Who?'

'China.'

Adam laughed.

'China?'

'Hear me out...' Dave spoke with enthusiasm as he explained, 'Every country is having a melt-down with stocks crashing, right?'

'Right. Including China.'

'But their stocks are on the up.'

Adam couldn't help but laugh again. 'On the up? Mate, I saw the fucking list showing how much the markets had crashed. They're hardly on the rise.'

'But everyone else is on the decline, they're still on the rise, if only by a little. We all go down and they go up. I'm telling you, they fucked us.'

Amused, Adam turned to Anett with a shit-eating grin on his face. 'This fucking guy.'

'I know. I'm kind of hoping that when the borders open up again, they still don't let him back into the country.'

'You'd miss me,' Dave said as he sat back. He turned to Chris and asked, 'What do you think?'

'Honestly who gives a fuck?' Chris swigged the whiskey. 'The world has gone to shit and we're driving to the fucking supermarket to do some shopping yet I just showed you cunts how easy it was to do the shopping... But, no, let's jump in the car and go and queue with every other fucking retard... Hey, don't forget to buy way too much toilet paper than we need too...' He drank. 'You're all fucking worried about this virus thing and yet, really, it could be the best thing to happen to us. Let it hit. Stop trying to delay the inevitable and let it kill half the cunts on the planet. We'd be in a better position afterwards. You want to talk conspiracy theories? Fuck it, okay. What if the powers that be decided to release this to kill off great numbers of the population. Less humans, less global warming. So, yeah, this was a fucking bioweapon but it was produced by our own governments as they struggle to protect our planet. Kill some of us with this fucking virus before we all kill ourselves by rotting our world. How's that?'

Dave paused a moment. 'No. I don't think that is right.'

Anett laughed. She knew that, tomorrow, Dave would come and tell her what Chris had said *but* it would be through his own point of view. In other words, Dave would pretend that it was *his* idea. Then, when the truth came out about the virus (if it hadn't already) Dave would be able to turn around and say how he had been right all along. *That was how his mind worked.*

'Kill most of the population?' Adam glanced back to Chris via the rear-view mirror. It was a quick look which went unnoticed but Chris knew he was talking to him.

'Fuck 'em.'

'Still upset about Anne leaving, huh?'

'Fuck you too,' Chris said.

Neither Dave nor Anett said anything. They knew Chris had recently been dumped but neither of them knew the actual story and, given his reaction now, they knew it wasn't their business.

'Got to suck being single now though, right? Hard to get out there and find a partner with every cunt wearing a mask. Probably pull a pig.' Adam laughed. 'Mind you, I met Anne so maybe a pig is a step up in your world.'

Just as the virus had sapped the energy from the world, so did Adam's comment from the already rocky atmosphere inr the car.

Chris took another sip of whiskey.

'Fuck that bitch. Plenty more fish in the sea.'

'Plenty more *mask wearing* fish in the sea.' Adam corrected him with perfect timing as, when they turned into the store's car park, there was such a woman standing by her car. Her nose and mouth covered with what looked like a surgical mask and, as they looked for a spot to park the car, she wasn't the only one wearing such attire.

5.

'This is insane,' Adam said. He was standing in the supermarket's entrance, with the others close-by. All of them were just staring ahead at the shoppers running around the store.

Despite usually being twenty-four hours, the store had closed overnight to give the staff the chance to restock everything. The local press had covered this event, urging people *not* to panic buy and to only take what they needed. The reiteration being loud and clear that the world was *not* running out of food. It was a message that most had missed apparently as people ran around the store like headless chickens.

'Look at this cunt,' Adam said, pointing towards a woman with a nod of his head.

This woman was pushing a trolley out in front of her with one hand and dragging another behind her with her other hand. Both trolleys were full of canned goods, pasta and - of course - toilet paper. At a glance Adam counted four large packs of toilet paper. Each pack contained twenty-four rolls.

'Unless you're Boris Johnson, there is no way you need that much fucking loo paper,' Adam said.

Dave was confused and asked, 'Why would Boris Johnson need so much?'

'Because the prick is full of shit.' Adam nodded towards the trolley and pointed out, 'Not even that would be enough paper for the crap that he spews.'

Dave laughed but mainly out of politeness. He'd long since learned that it was easier to avoid conversations about politics, especially in foreign countries where his opinion would be as welcome as a fart in a spacesuit. And, by avoiding such conversations, it made for less arguments.

'Okay so… Split up or stay together?'

Chris walked off and, as he did so, he called back, 'Fuck this shit. I'm going to find the booze.'

Anett answered on behalf of her and Dave, 'I think we should stick together. Probably easier.'

Adam nodded. 'Okay then. Let's get this done.' He took a step forward only to be stopped by Dave grabbing his arm.

'You don't think we'll need more than that?' Dave was making reference to the basket Adam was carrying.

'No, Dave, I don't. Because we're not cunts like these people. We'll just get what we need.'

'But there are a few of us in the house.'

'Then you can get a basket too, Dave.'

Anett asked, 'Should I get one?'

'Let's just hurry up, yeah? Probably already missed out on toilet rolls.'

6.

As Tessa approached the supermarket car park she saw an empty carrier bag blowing across the tarmac like some kind of manufactured tumbleweed.

She hesitated for a moment, trying to catch sight of anyone else in or around the huge building. A few people hurried from their cars and the car park itself seemed pretty full suggesting that, inside the store, it was bedlam.

The walk from her flat had taken her about twenty minutes and it was now approaching noon, the sky above her heavy with clouds. The rain at least had eased and as she walked on she was beginning to wonder why she'd even bothered with the trip to the supermarket. There'd be nothing left worth having by now anyway. The shelves would have been stripped clean of anything that she really wanted but she made the trek anyway. It was as much to free herself temporarily from the confines of her flat.

Too many hours spent in that cramped space didn't help her. She needed the freedom, no matter how fleeting it might be. Or how risky.

As she moved closer to the main doors of the supermarket, she slowed her pace slightly.

If the virus was as easily communicable as everyone thought then wasn't she taking a huge chance just by coming here? It was airborne. That meant it was all around her now didn't it? Its effects even more concentrated in the confines of a supermarket where others who might be infected were walking about. She sucked in a deep breath.

A contaminated breath?

She coughed involuntarily.

'You should be wearing a mask.'

The words came from the right of her and she turned warily, wondering who had spoken them.

A heavily built man with a greying beard was clambering out of his car nearby.

'If you're coughing you shouldn't be going in there,' he grunted, walking past her. 'You could infect other people.'

Tessa wondered if she should explain to him that she wasn't infected (well, not as far as she knew) but that it was just one, single, innocent cough. A clearing of the throat. Not a sign that she was carrying the virus. But was she? She hadn't been tested. She had no way of knowing for sure. No one did unless they'd been tested. She hadn't felt ill. She hadn't had a fever. She hadn't succumbed to coughing fits lasting in excess of an hour (one of the things to look out for according to the experts on the TV). To her knowledge, she was still healthy.

'You shouldn't be so selfish,' the big man continued, waddling across the car park just ahead of her.

Tessa thought about telling him to mind his own business but then decided against it. He looked like the kind who might shout back at her and the last thing she wanted was a row with a stranger. He glanced back over his shoulder at her as he reached the automatic doors of the supermarket which whirred open to admit him.

Tessa passed through the open doors too, surprised at how cold it felt inside the supermarket.

Normally the place was relatively warm and welcoming but today it seemed somehow alien. The lights above her seemed to be unusually bright, bathing those below in a cold white glow that seemed to reflect off the polished tiles of the floor. The fact that there was a Robbie Williams song spewing from the speakers didn't help.

Tessa found a trolley and wheeled it into the heart of the supermarket.

As she turned towards the fruit and vegetable section she could see that the first few aisles were bare.

Her journey around the huge building revealed that much of the rest of it was in the same state.

Tinned vegetables, rice, pasta, flour, eggs. All were gone. Gobbled up by the human locusts that had descended earlier. She sighed wearily as she moved up and down the aisles, trying to decide if she really needed some packets of vegetable rice. She picked them up anyway. Why not? Any kind of food was better than nothing and she knew she was running low back at the flat.

She scooped up some frozen peas too and some madeira cake, managing to snatch it off the shelf just before a woman in her forties who glared at her as if she'd just spat in her face.

There were more than two dozen people in the supermarket, some similarly desperate as herself, others who strode around as if they owned the building, scanning the shelves. Some merely swept items from the shelves directly into their trolleys. Tessa wondered what anyone would really need that much drinking chocolate for. Especially when milk was in short supply.

As she turned a corner into another aisle she caught sight of the big man who'd spoken to her in the car park.

He was busy placing packets of soup into his trolley, piling pot noodle and jars of pickled onions on top of them.

Tessa walked briskly past him but he didn't see her or didn't recognise her. She really didn't care which.

He broke wind loudly as she passed, his only acknowledgement of her presence.

She tutted dismissively and collected some milk before turning into the next aisle.

As she did, she heard the shouting. And she froze when she saw what was ahead of her.

7.

There were four of them.

Strung across the aisle as if they were barring anyone else from walking down its narrow confines.

All around the same age, Tessa thought. All in their teens or early twenties. All dressed similarly in what could have been a uniform. Tracksuits or jeans and big, thick coats as if they were protecting themselves against sub zero temperatures. One of them, the one nearest to her, was pushing a trolley that was piled high with sweets, chocolate bars, fizzy drink and alcohol.

It was he who looked at her. His gaze travelling slowly up and down as he took in every detail before him.

One of the others joined him in looking at her and she noticed that he was chewing on a piece of liquorice he'd pulled from one of the packets he'd taken from the shelves. He chewed noisily, occasionally wiping his nose with the back of his hand.

He and one of the others were throwing a packet of dried milk back and forth as if it were a ball. When it split and sent white powder spilling all over the floor the group dissolved into waves of raucous laughter.

Tessa hesitated but realised that the little group were in the aisle where the teabags and the coffee were. Things she actually *needed*.

Go around, come back when they've gone.

She was about to move when she saw the big man from the car park entering the aisle from the other end. He walked purposefully down the aisle, picking up boxes and packets, shoving them into his trolley it seemed without even caring what was inside them.

Two of the youths turned to look at him as he bustled past them. The big man glanced down at the spilled white powder on the floor and shook his head.

'Did you do that?' he said to the nearest youth.

'Who wants to know?' one of the youths grunted, smiling at his companions.

'You shouldn't be wasting stuff like that,' the big man told him, shaking his head.

'Fuck off, you fat cunt,' another spat.

'What did you say?' the big man snapped, glaring at him.

The youth stood his ground.

'I said, fuck off you fat cunt,' he repeated, enunciating each word as if he were speaking to a foreigner or a deaf person. 'Did you hear me that time?'

The others laughed.

One of them pulled open a box and threw a tea bag at the big man, who gripped the handle of his trolley so hard his knuckles turned white.

'Did you hear him?' one of the girls from the group echoed, taking a step closer to the big man.

He turned to look briefly at the young woman who was grinning widely.

'You've got a lot of stuff in there, haven't you?' the first lad grunted, pointing into the big man's trolley. 'You look like you need to be cutting down on fucking food, not shovelling it in. Fat fucker.'

Again they laughed.

The big man reversed his trolley slightly. There was no point starting anything with these bloody kids. He knew what they were like when there was a gang of them. They only shot their fucking mouths off *because* there was a gang of them.

'Yeah, go on, fuck off,' the lad called, waving the man away. He hawked loudly and spat on the floor. The lump of phlegm landed inches from the trolley.

Another chorus of laughter greeted this.

Tessa sucked in a deep breath, turned and wheeled her own trolley away. As she did she heard a loud wolf whistle from behind her.

She swallowed hard when she heard the sound, not turning as she might normally have to smile or rebuke. She just wanted to be away from this little group.

'You don't have to run away,' one of them called. 'We can help you.'

More laughter.

'Yeah, we'll help you,' another called.

Tessa walked more quickly now, ducking into the next aisle, wanting to be anywhere but close to these youths.

She bent low over her trolley and pushed it towards the line of checkouts up ahead.

Some of the other shoppers glanced at her, wondering why she was almost running between the aisles. Tessa glanced over her shoulder to ensure no one was following her but, another burst of laughter assured her that the youths were still in the aisle where she'd left them. She slowed her pace a little and then took up position in the queue of shoppers who were waiting patiently at the nearest check out.

Tessa glanced around again but there was still no sign of the little group. She saw the big man lumbering along, now adding washing up sponges to his trolley as he moved methodically up and down the aisles.

A security guard with greying hair and attired in a red jacket bearing the name badge Steve Matthewman, walked into view behind one of the tills and stood there with his hands clasped behind his back. When he noticed that a woman had placed four packs of toilet roll on the conveyor belt before him he stepped forward wagging one index finger officiously.

'Only two packs of toilet roll per person, madam,' he said, now shaking his head too.

'I need those,' the woman protested.

'So do other people,' Matthewman informed her, reaching for the packs and removing them from the black, moving belt.

'I've got three kids at home,' the woman hissed. 'What are they supposed to wipe their arses on? Sand paper?'

'Two packs per customer,' Matthewman reminded her.

'Fucking jobsworth,' the woman grunted, glaring at him briefly before placing some other items on the conveyor belt.

'And I don't have to put up with language like that,' Matthewman told her. He pointed to a sign above the till that proclaimed:

OUR STAFF ARE HERE TO HELP. WE WILL NOT TOLERATE ABUSE TOWARDS THEM.

'Piss off,' the woman muttered to herself.

Matthewman turned and walked away, moving to the head of the next till. Tessa glanced at him then began placing her own meagre shopping haul on the conveyor belt.

When she reached the till the woman who was seated there scanned each item dutifully, smiling at Tessa from behind a protective face mask. The name on her overall proclaimed:

HERE TO HELP YOU
SOPHIE HALL
HAVE A NICE DAY

Normally, Tessa would have found the sentiment nauseatingly insincere but, today, it didn't bother her in the slightest. She asked for a carrier bag and began pushing her shopping inside it.

'Card or cash,' Sophie Hall asked from behind her protective mask.

'Card,' Tessa said, producing a credit card from her purse. She waved it towards the screen of the contactless device and listened for the beep that would announce it had been approved. It didn't come.

She was about to say something when she caught sight of movement out of her eye corner.

The youths she'd seen earlier were barrelling towards the next checkout, one of them pushing the heavily laden trolley they were using as if he were driving a chariot towards waiting enemies.

She turned her back towards them.

'Your card has been refused,' Sophie Hall said, her voice slightly muffled by the mask she wore. 'Have you got cash? Or another card?'

'Sorry,' Tessa said, pulling another card from her purse and pushing it towards the machine, inserting it this time instead of waving it at the screen. She popped in her pin number and waited, relieved when the payment was accepted.

The next person in the queue tutted and sighed, not keen on waiting too much longer. She glanced sheepishly at them and tried not to meet their gaze. Why were some people so impatient, she wondered?

At the next till, Dave, Chris, Anett and Adam were emptying their trolley contents onto the conveyor belt.

Steve Matthewman wandered towards them, gazing at what they were putting on the moving black material. When he saw the bottle of Jack Daniels, from Chris, he stepped forward.

'You'll need I.d if you're buying that,' he said, looking at Chris Whiteman.

Chris eyed him contemptuously.

'And what if I haven't got it?' he said, softly.

'Then you can't buy that,' Matthewman informed him, pointing at the bottle of Jack Daniels.

'Then I'll have to *take* it,' Chris grunted. 'Are you going to stop me, old man?' Chris noticed Tessa was watching him. He smiled at her and cockily flashed her a wink. She immediately looked away to concentrate on her own tasks. Chris hesitated a moment and then turned back to the man, challenging him further. 'Well?'

'Just leave it,' Adam said, frustrated.

'Yeah. Fine. Fuck you all.' With the effects of the earlier drinking taking a hold, Chris stormed away from both his friends and the happy worker, Steve Matthewman. 'Fuck. You. All.'

'Should I go after him?'

'Just let him go,' Adam said. 'Drunk prick.'

There was a smash from further down in the store, followed by more loud laughter. Steve rolled his eyes. *Fucking world is going crazy.* He headed in the direction of the noise.

8

Tessa pushed the last of her shopping into her carrier bag and turned, aware that she had to pass the security guard and the gang when she left.

A hush had fallen over the queues of shoppers as a number of them craned their necks to see what developed at the till where the youths were congregated.

The tension was almost palpable. It was like someone was clenching their fists more and more tightly with each passing second.

"I need to see all your I.d.," Matthewman said, glancing at the youths. *I need to see your I.D seemingly being his catchphrase.*

"You don't have to do what this cunt says," the youngest looking lad hissed, looking at his companions. "Do we?"

His older friend ignored him, his gaze fixed on the security guard.

The woman sitting at the till had moved her chair back slightly as if she was anxious to make a quick get-away should trouble start.

Tessa also took a step back, her route out now blocked by Matthewman who was trying to ensure that the youths didn't suddenly bolt for the exits or, if they did, that he had a fighting chance of catching at least one of them.

"Your I.d.," he repeated.

"Please," the eldest of the lads chided. "Say please and you can have it."

"If you don't show me you can't buy that alcohol," the security man insisted, trying to keep his voice even despite his mounting agitation.

"Say please."

The security man squeezed his jaws together tightly and held out his hand for the I.d.

One of the girls pushed hers forward reluctantly. So did her friend. The two lads held onto theirs.

Matthewman gestured towards the boys again.

"The I.d," he persisted.

The eldest lad pulled his free slowly, looked at it for a moment then tossed it on the floor in front of the security man.

"You want it, it's down there," he said, contemptuously.

"Pick it up," Matthewman said.

"*You* pick it up, you old cunt," he hissed. "*You* want it."

The two of them faced each other like gunfighters in some long forgotten Western street. Neither moved.

"For God's sake," Tessa sighed and she dropped to one knee, scooped up the I.d. Card and handed it to Matthewman.

She looked at each of them in turn and then headed for the exit.

Behind her she could hear words being exchanged but what was being said she neither knew or cared. She made her way towards the automatic doors, wanting to be outside once again. Wanting to be away from the supermarket and those inside it. The prospect of being alone in her flat again suddenly seemed like a very enticing thought now that the world had clearly gone to shit.

"Satisfied?" The lad said, watching as Matthewman looked at the identification card.

The security man pushed the I.d card across the metal till area and stepped backwards.

"We'll need a bag for our shopping," the lad said to the woman at the till. "And you can pack it for us too."

He smiled crookedly, watching as the till attendant pushed the shopping into the carrier bag, her hands shaking slightly. When the bag was full she pushed it towards her *customer* who snatched it up.

The little group walked slowly towards the exit doors, watched the whole way by Matthewman who moved towards them, wanting to ensure they left the building without any trouble. His heart was beating a little faster than it should have been but he continued tracking the group, breathing an inward sigh of relief when they finally reached the doors and moved out into the rain spattered day beyond.

9.

BEFORE

Anne Lambley called up the stairs again, 'Chris?' She paused a moment, listening for him to answer. Her heart raced at the prospect of hearing him, and not in a way suggesting *excitement*. 'Are you home?'

Silence.

Slowly, she let out an audible sigh of relief before she set her handbag down. If she was doing this, she wouldn't have long. Quickly, she ran up the stairs towards the bedroom she'd shared with Chris for the last five years. Five years and only one of those could have been classed as *happy*. This... Running... This had been a long time coming and no less than what he deserved. If anything, he was getting off light after all he had put her through with his childish mind games and constant head-fucks.

In the bedroom: She ran over to the closet and opened it up. The last time she had been home alone, she had already packed a bag of clothes; the essentials like underwear and a few different outfits just to see her through. Everything else he could keep as most of it was tarnished with unpleasant memories of him anyway; this once nice man so bitterly twisted with his ongoing consumption of alcohol.

Anne grabbed the bag and froze on the spot and what she thought was the sound of a key sliding into a lock.

The only sound now was that of her thumping heart.

'Hello?'

No answer.

Anne closed the closet door and hurried from the room and back down the landing towards the stairs. This was the *dangerous* part. If she were to meet him coming in, as she was leaving with the bag, she knew she wouldn't be met with joy and laughter. Especially as he had already sounded as though he was in a bad mood when she had spoken to him earlier in the day.

Just be quick, she thought.

At the bottom of the stairs: An unwanted memory flashed to mind which saw Anne looking down at herself in a crumpled heap. Her body twisted at an awkward angle. Fear in her eyes. The eyes themselves staring up to the top of the stairs where *he* was standing. He was drunk, swaying there with an almost empty bottle to hand. There was no remorse on his face that day but she knew it would be there come morning, when he would beg her forgiveness. She would give it, as she always did, but no lessons would be learned from either of them. Nothing changed. He would spend a few days being nice to her and then the cycle would start again; he would begin drinking, get angry for whatever reason and - then - he would take it out on her. *Nothing changed.*

Anne shook the memory from mind and grabbed her handbag from where she'd earlier set it down. *He deserves this*, she thought as she hurried to the front door.

As Anne pulled the door open, a ray of sunshine hit her face, immediately warming her from the cold memories. This was her fresh start; a better life was waiting.

NOW

Chris was standing outside the supermarket, pissed that the security guard dared to challenge him, when he saw Tessa for the second time. He was leaning back on the wall, smoking a cigarette, when she came out with her shopping bags. Just as he had thought when he first saw her in the supermarket, he couldn't help but think how similar she looked to Anne. Had it not been for the fact he knew Anne was an only child, he would have thought this woman was her damned twin.

At first he had just watched her as she crossed the car park, heading for the narrow pathway leading to the housing estates. He didn't consciously *think* to follow her and yet that was exactly what he was doing; one foot after the other and with his brain asking what the hell he was doing with each step. *Blame the alcohol.*

Up ahead Tessa walked on.

She had no idea she was being followed and neither was she the only one oblivious to what was happening around her.

10

'Where the fuck is he?'

Adam was sitting in the driver's seat of his car. Anett was next to him and, like Adam, she was looking all around the car park through the closed windows for any sign of Chris.

Adam put his phone to his ear again, having already called Chris's number. For the second time, it went through to voicemail.

'Chris? Where the fuck are you? I thought we were all going back to play some FIFA? Give me a text or something, yeah? I don't really want to sit in the fucking car like a lemon all day if you're not coming back.' He hung the call up and tossed the phone down into the car's cup-holder.

Dave leaned forward, poking his head through to the front of the car once again. 'Maybe he went back in looking for us?'

'He knew where we were. It's not like we were walking around the store.'

'Then maybe he decided he wouldn't be a prick about the I.D and went back to get his alcohol?' Dave shrugged. 'Always possible.'

Anett laughed. 'That security guy though. Did you see him? He was trying to get some others to hand over their I.D when we left too.'

Adam smirked. 'I did notice. Fucking jobsworth.'

'Maybe he gets a bonus for collecting I.Ds?'

'Or maybe he's just a twat,' Adam suggested. Adam sighed. Without turning, he asked Dave, 'Did you want to go and see if you can spot him? We can't just sit here all fucking day.'

With no warning, the rear door of the car was suddenly yanked open.

'Finally,' Adam said, presuming it was Chris arriving from wherever. 'Where the fuck did...'

'Want to give me and my friends a lift?'

It wasn't Chris.

Dave span round to see who had climbed into the car next to him. It was one of the youths from the supermarket. Adam twisted in his seat too.

'What the fuck are you doing? Get the fuck out of my car!'

The youth turned to Dave and smiled. 'Hi.'

There was a bang from the other side of the car, on Anett's window. She jumped and turned to see one of the other youths standing there, leaning down and staring straight through the window at her. Just as the other one was smiling, so was she but - it wasn't a friendly greeting given the blackness of her shark-like eyes.

'Seriously, mate, you want to get the fuck out of my car right now.'

'No. I don't think so.'

The passenger door of the car was yanked open.

Alarmed, Adam asked, 'Who the fuck are you?'

A bang from the bonnet of the car stole his attention away from the stranger seated in the rear. The other lad was standing by the front of the car, leaning on the bonnet with a grin on his face.

Adam slammed his clenched fist on the horn and shouted, 'Get the fuck off my car, you fucking prick.' The instruction was ignored as the guy just casually laughed at him.

The lad in the back leaned forward and slapped Adam upside the head. 'Oi. Cut that shit out. As I was saying, my friends and I need a lift and you're going to give it to us. Okay?'

'I'm not going anywhere with you,' Adam said defiantly. 'Get the fuck out of my car.'

The lad, Darren Edmett, smiled. 'You sure you want to fucking do this?'

'Mate, you're about a second away from me getting out of this car and kicking the shit out of you.'

'That a fact?'

'Yeah. That is a fact.'

Darren shrugged. Then, in an instant, he pulled a knife from within his jacket and plunged it directly into Dave's side. Dave, in turn, screamed out in pain as both Anett and Adam screamed in shock.

The door opened on Dave's side of the car and another youth, Kevin Freeman, leaned in. He grabbed Dave around his neck and yanked him from the car. With blood pumping from his side, Dave didn't put up much of a fight as he was unceremoniously dumped on the cold, wet concrete of the carpark.

Kevin climbed into the rear of the vehicle and slid across the back seat, next to Darren, as he cleaned the blood off his blade. One of the girls, Sharon Freeman, climbed in and sat next to Kevin. She brought their shopping with her and set it on her own lap.

'What have you fucking done?' Adam asked, not so much fearful for his life but for the life of his friend. He sat there, shaking, unsure whether he should jump from the car to see if Dave was okay or whether he should remain seated.

'I've freed up some cunt's seat so my friends could fit in here,' Darren said with a wink. 'You're gonna give us a lift to where we want to fucking go now, okay?' He paused a moment and turned his attention to Anett. 'You not going to let my friend sit down?'

Outside the car, standing next to the passenger door, Billy Smith suddenly pulled a blade too. Before Anett had a chance to react, he leaned in and rammed it up through her chin. The blade pierced the skin and pushed through her mouth, pricking the roof of it in the process. Anett let out the weirdest of sounds as Adam once again screamed in shock. When Billy pulled the blade out,

Anett immediately raised her hands to the bleeding wound in an effort to stem the blood.

Calmly, Billy put his knife away - tucking it down the front of his belt - and then leaned back in to undo Anett's seat-belt. With her free now, he grabbed her and yanked her out of the seat before letting her drop to the ground close to where Dave still writhed around in agony.

Billy sat and pulled the door shut. He smiled at Adam who was just staring at him with panic all over his now pale face. Adam looked away. His mind was torn; run from the car and hope they just take the vehicle and leave him be, or do as they ask and hope they let him go at the end of it. A little voice in his head: *They won't let you go whatever you choose. All you can do is delay the inevitable.*

'So this fucking car start itself or you need to do any-thing to help it out?' Kevin laughed from the back. His laughter stopped and he punched up against the roof of the car. 'Let's fucking go already!'

Adam hesitated. He leaned towards the key, sticking from the ignition, and twisted it. The engine stuttered into life.

'Where am I driving?'

11

BEFORE

To start with, people in the United Kingdom acted with careful thought when the virus came to light. People seemed more compassionate of one another, offering the vulnerable some help here and there, and the country seemed to stand together as if to say, *We will not be beaten*. Such was the solidarity of the people that the Prime Minister even made a passing comment, thanking each and every one of the people for doing their part.

It was never going to last.

With more and more rules and regulations put into place, people started to go stir crazy. Bars, pubs, restaurants and smaller shops all shut up shop, as per the government's instruction, and people were told to stay in their homes unless going out for food, or to a doctor's appointment. Stuck at home with their partners and, thanks to the schools being closed, their children - all of whom were complaining about being bored - tempers began to rise.

People would ignore the curfews and sneak out, doing all they could to avoid the authorities. Some would just want a walk and "fresh air" and others would be looking to cause trouble after something in their brain clicked, *It's the end of the world so why live by normal rules*?

Soon after people would sit in their homes and listen to the sirens wailing through the night air as police rushed to break-ins (both for businesses and domestic settings), paramedics sped to those who were battling chronic illness or struggling against the virus and fire-fighters charged to foolish acts of arson, initiated by the frustrated and braindead.

Those living in the main cities, high in their tower blocks, could best see the country for what it truly was when the sun went down and blackness fell. This wasn't the world people were used to anymore and some (most) doubted whether we would ever get that world back or whether this was it now, and it would continue spiralling towards uncontrollable depths of depravity.

The good would hunker down at night, locking themselves in and barricading the doors and windows to the properties they were confined to whilst the bad made no such efforts to protect themselves; they just made their antisocial plans to go and take what didn't truly belong to them.

The crimes started small but, as the days went on, they continued to escalate as the bad element realised that the authorities were losing their control of the situation with forces spread too thin.

*

'I'm going to miss this shit,' Billy said as he pulled his jeans back up and fastened his thick leather belt around his waist. He reached into his pocket and grabbed a squashed pack of cigarettes. He tutted when he opened the pack and saw the vast majority of smokes had been bent back. 'Fuck sake.' He tossed the pack to the floor and walked over to where Darren's pants were lying. He picked them up and ferreted in the pockets until he found Darren's own supply.

Darren didn't give a shit. He was too pre-occupied with the woman, as she struggled under him, to worry about whether Billy took the last of his cigarettes.

'Fucking stop moving.' Darren followed his order up with a short, sharp jab to the woman's face. Her nose immediately split and started to stream blood. The pain stung so bad that her eyes watered almost instantly. The blow had the desired effect though and her body went limp.

Darren squeezed his hard cock into her tight vagina which was only wet thanks to Billy's hot spunk dribbling from within.

'Fuck…'

Joanne Ormshaw, Joe to her friends, had come home to what she had expected to be an empty house. A nurse in the nearby hospital, it had been a long, miserable shift trying to deal with the influx of patients. All she had wanted to do was get in and crash out on the sofa with crap on the television and a Pot Noodle to hand. Sure it wasn't the healthiest of meals but after the day she'd had, it would suffice.

Her evening plans changed the moment she walked from hallway to living room and found the gang of youths going through her things, looking for something (anything) to steal. She screamed, and turned to run, but both her cries and escape attempts were cut short with a heavy rugby tackle.

Both petrified and dazed, Joanne was flipped onto her back by Billy. She begged for him to let her go but he refused. Instead he just smiled down at her and reached up under her work uniform before ripping her white, cotton panties down. She started to cry as he raised them to his face and inhaled deeply.

'Fragrant.'

Darren came hard, firing his load deep inside Joanne's aching cunt. The moment his prick stopped the orgasmic twitches, he pulled out with an accompanying mixture of both his and Billy's spunk. Joanne just laid there. Her tears had stopped now. She turned her head to the side to look at any part of the room that didn't have any of *them* standing there watching her.

'Give me one of them,' Darren said with a gesture to his own pack of cigarettes which were still in Billy's hand. Billy tossed the pack over. As Darren got a smoke out, he asked, 'What are you going to miss.'

'This.' Billy gestured towards the room and to the broken girl. 'All this.'

'What? You want to stay here forever?'

'No, you fucking idiot. Days like this. What we're fucking doin'…'

'I didn't realise we were gonna be stopping?'

'You know they'll be calling in the army soon, right? Soon we'll have those cunts traipsing around the place like they fucking own it and you think it will be easy to get around and do this? Nah. Don't fucking think so. We'll all be locked in. Who knows, it'll probably get to a stage where they see people out and about and just fucking shoot 'em. Anything to stop the spread of the virus.'

'It won't come to that, prick.'

'You're so sure? Even if it don't… The army's still comin'.'

Darren laughed.

'What's so fucking funny?'

'You worry too much. This all has to stop? Fine. We'll just have to make the fucking most of it now, huh?'

Darren jumped up and left the room.

'Where you goin'?'

Billy stood there and, as he did so, he could hear random drawers opening and closing from the other room, along with the clattering of what he guessed to be cutlery.

Darren walked back in with two kitchen knives; one in each hand. He held one out to Billy and said, 'Here.'

'What you doin'?' Billy took the knife.

'What does it fucking look like? I'm making the most our freedom.' He laughed and turned his attention to the battered woman on the floor. Billy stood there and watched as Darren knelt down to the woman.

'Darren?'

'Watch.'

With no further words, Darren thrust up into Joanne's pussy with the knife. Her cunt swallowed the whole blade as she screamed out in sheer agony. The pitch in her scream went up a notch as Darren twisted the knife with a flick of his wrist. He pulled the knife out and stabbed straight back up for a second time. Same again, a little flick of his wrist to twist the blade.

Billy laughed and joined his friend next to Joanne as she writhed around in pain.

Showing off his yellow nicotine-stained teeth as he continued grinning, Billy started repeatedly puncturing Joanne's stomach with the blade Darren had given him. Joanne coughed dark red blood from her mouth as she fruitlessly tried to push them away with heavy, weak arms.

Even after she stopped moving, Billy continued stabbing his sharp blade down into her ruptured gut. With every blow, he laughed.

Darren sat back and wiped his own dirty blade clean on Joanne's bare leg. Smiling, he asked, 'So where next?'

12.

NOW

Adam drove in silence. All they had told him was to get on the motorway and in what direction to drive. He had no idea where they were driving him to, what they wanted or what they were going to do when they got to wherever. All he knew was that he had left his friends lying in a car park and that, if someone hadn't found them, they would most likely be dead by now.

Still, it was hard to cry with fear and adrenaline running through his veins.

'Show me the picture again,' Kevin said to Billy from the rear.

Adam flinched as Billy started ferreting in his pocket. He pulled out his mobile and unlocked it with a press of his thumb. With one eye on the road, Adam tried to see what Billy was searching for.

Billy was going through his photos but too fast for Adam to really make anything out.

'Here,' he said.

Kevin leaned forward from the back and took Billy's phone from him. He looked at the screen and started to laugh.

'That is fucking sick.' He turned to his sister and showed her the screen. 'Look.'

'Fuck off. I don't want to see it.'

'Whatever.'

On the phone was a series of pictures; namely of what remained of Joanne. Close-up shots, medium shots, long shots. The picture loaded up now, for Kevin's benefit, was a snap of her pussy. It hung there resembling a take-away kebab; slithers of meat dangling in bloodied tatters. The blood, nothing more than ketchup. Darren and Billy's cum? Sour cream.

'Give it,' Billy said as he reached back for his phone.

'You gotta send me that shit, man.'

Billy snatched his phone back.

'I don't fucking think so.'

'You should fucking delete it,' Darren said.

'Why? You delete yours?'

Both Billy and Darren laughed.

'So we gonna do another, yeah? I vote we come back later and fuck that security guard cunt up,' Kevin suggested. He was disappointed he hadn't been part of the action the other night but, he'd been stuck at home and unable to get out.

'You don't shit on your own doorstep,' Darren said.

'You fucking joking? That bitch lived less than ten minutes from yours,' Kevin said, referring to Joanne.

'Yeah but she was a bitch and so I made an exception.'

'The security guard was a prick so make another,' Kevin pushed.

'Fuck that shit. We got a car now. Our own personal driver to take us around.' Darren leaned forward over the driver's seat and patted the top of Adam's head. Adam said nothing.

'Fucking road trip!' Kevin shouted excitedly.

Darren leaned round to look at Sharon. 'Bitch, how's about a little road-head?'

Sharon flipped Darren the finger and told him, 'Billy might be up for it but you'd have to ask him nicely.'

Kevin laughed until Darren responded by punching him on the leg.

Adam pushed his foot down on the accelerator in the hope of attracting the police, not that there were many other cars on the road right now. He couldn't help but wonder what would happen if anyone did see them speeding around, or even if they had noticed what had happened before they left the carpark. The world had gone to shit. Would anyone have even tried to help or would they have turned a blind eye fearful of the repercussions, not just from the gang but the possibility that one of the people they were trying to help was carrying the virus. *Sorry, I can't help. Social distancing.*

It was too late to wish he had listened to the government and locked himself away in his house now. All Adam could do was go for the ride and hope he made it to the other end.

'Fuck! I know where we can go!' Kevin was grinning in the rear of the car. A smiled that stretched from ear to ear and highlighted a missing tooth, lost in a fight over a year ago. He addressed Adam, 'Oi. This shit-hole got a sat nav system?'

Adam pretended not to hear.

'Answer him, you cunt.'

'Yes. It does,' Adam said.

'Load that cunt up. I got an address for you.' Kevin laughed. Sharon laughed along with him. She knew Kevin well and could already tell what was on his mind.

Adam's mind drifted to Chris. Maybe he saw these fucks get in the car? Maybe he was calling for help? Maybe the police were out, already looking for them?

Maybe?

13.

There was something lying in the middle of the pathway up ahead but Tessa couldn't quite make out what it was. She slowed her pace slightly, not sure if the misshapen bundle was an animal or some clothes. A slight breeze blew and Tessa shivered. The bundle ahead of her moved slightly.

Didn't it?

Was it an animal? Injured perhaps. Unable to move?

Tessa slowed down to a virtual stop, squinting to try and see exactly what was ahead of her. She didn't know why she felt so nervous. If it was an animal she could walk past it. If it was a bundle of clothes she could by pass them. Although one thought did strike her a little harder than normal.

Was the virus carried by animals? Could it remain active on discarded articles?

Was what lay ahead of her like a booby trap in a demolished building or a mine on a battlefield?

She muttered something under her breath, annoyed with herself for her indecision. Whatever it was, that was lying in the middle of the deserted pathway, it wasn't going to hurt her.

Was it?

These feelings of paranoia had multiplied to a ridiculous degree during the last few months. As hysteria in the media had exploded about the virus, people's mindsets had changed irrevocably. How much was actually known about the threat? (Answer; very little). Much of the fear had been built up through social media, flames of concern fanned happily by the media who seemed determined to elevate the virus to the level of Ebola or Bubonic plague. Which it quite clearly wasn't. Couple that with the innate stupidity of some members of the general public and the greed and selfishness of too many more and it looked certain that *people* would kill more people than any barely understood virus could strike down.

Tessa sucked in a deep breath, wondering why she was suddenly engaging in some kind of internal debate rather than just making her way home.

She walked on towards the object ahead, her expression changing as she finally realised what it was.

It was a supermarket carrier bag and, as she drew closer, she realised that it was full of shopping.

What the hell was it doing there? Had someone dropped it and run off? It couldn't have been dropped without the owner noticing it. Tessa took a couple of steps nearer.

Had it been left there deliberately? Was it some kind of strange and unfathomable joke?

She looked around. The walkway was fringed by low hedges and trees and for fleeting seconds, Tessa wondered if someone had left the bag there and was now hiding and watching to see what occurred when someone came across it.

Surely not?

She walked across to the hedge and peered over. No one there. No one hiding. No jokers waiting for a reaction. Not that she could see anyway. She went back to the bag and looked at it more closely. There wasn't a great deal inside it. Some tins of carrots. Some coffee.

But, there, jammed beneath a bag of Brussels sprouts lay the true treasure.

A large bag of rice.

Tessa was only too aware that she was out of the precious commodity. It was tempting.

She reached towards the bag but then quickly withdrew her hand.

What if the bag was rigged like a bomb?

Oh, for God's sake. Get a fucking grip. This is the world in the grip of Corona Virus, not a terrorist playground.

Nevertheless, she hesitated, gazing down at the bag of rice in the same way a diabetic might look at life saving insulin. She only needed to reach in, grab the bag and drop it in with her own shopping. Then, another ten minutes and she'd be home. Job done.

Still Tessa hesitated.

She prodded the bag with the toe of her boot, moving back slightly, just in case.

Nothing happened.

She sucked in another deep breath, steeled herself and shot a hand into the bag, her heart thudding against her ribs.

As she pulled the rice free, the bag fell to one side with a rattle and Tessa jumped, wondering if she'd activated the booby trap. Needless to say, she hadn't. She held the rice triumphantly for a moment then slipped it into her own shopping bag. Mission accomplished. She smiled. A little embarrassed and annoyed with herself for being so jumpy but also delighted with her acquisition.

She set off for home feeling like a hunter who'd just bagged a killer lion.

About two hundred yards behind her, Chris Whiteman ducked back behind one side of the underpass, ensuring that she wouldn't see him if she looked around. He stayed hidden among the bushes and trees for a moment longer then stepped out onto the walkway once again.

His footsteps echoed loudly around him as he walked beneath the underpass, glancing at the grafitti on either side as he moved through.

Above him the road that ran across it was silent. Deserted. Just like most of the way had been that led back from the supermarket.

He passed houses that also remained silent despite most of them having self isolating people inside. The weak sunlight reflected off the windows. A gleam in blind eyes.

Whiteman glanced ahead again and realised that Tessa was turning a corner. He sped up slightly, not wanting to lose her. It was easier to keep track in the confines of deserted streets but it also made him more visible and he didn't want that.

It would have been better if it had been dark. He could have melted into the shadows. The daylight made him too visible. Too noticeable. But, then again, who was going to be looking out of their window now? Everyone was glued to their TV waiting for the latest news of the virus or reading or doing whatever the fuck they did when they were confined to their homes for Christ alone knew how long.

Whiteman walked on, looking more closely at some of the houses. They were impressive looking buildings.

Worth a lot of money. He had no doubt that what was inside them was valuable too. When all this bullshit was over and people were out and about again it might be worth revisiting some of these dwellings. He smiled. Many had alarms outside but those were easily dealt with. He'd never had problems with alarms before.

He began imagining what he might be able to steal from some of these houses when the time was right.

But then he realised that his quarry was getting too far ahead and he again increased his speed slightly.

Fuck what was inside these houses. At the moment he had other things on his mind.

He saw Tessa approaching another turn in the road and he realised she was making for the large building ahead of her. That must be where she lived, he mused.

The journey was almost over.

The fun was just about to begin.

14

Tessa fumbled in her pocket for her keys and pushed the smallest of them into the lock, stepping into the hallway of the flats.

To both sides of her were mailboxes and she checked hers, not expecting anything to be inside.

Posting of letters and packaging had been stopped two weeks earlier due to the fact that the Covid-19 Virus supposedly lived on the surfaces of things and could easily live on envelopes or parcels. None of this had actually been proven but, as seemed to be the habit with the media, scaremongering and the spreading of fear would do just as well if hard news was in short supply.

She was surprised to find a small slip of paper in the mail box.

It proclamed;

*** ATTENTION ALL LOCAL RESIDENTS***
COMMUNITY SUPPORT GROUP (COVID19)

Beneath that blaring headline was a few lines about the virus and how some concerned citizens were prepared to help those who were vulnerable, elderly or living alone. There were phone numbers that could be called if anyone needed help.

Tessa thought this was a fine sentiment but exactly how the concerned citizens were going to find the food that the vulnerable, elderly or others needed was a different matter. Did they have special supermarkets they visited that had stocks of essential food others didn't? Did they know pharmacies where paracetamol wasn't as scarce as rocking horse shit? Did they have contacts that no one else knew about?

Tessa folded the piece of paper and slipped it into her jacket.

This was the kind of thing you didn't hear about as much on the news programmes. When the virus had first struck a few altruistic souls had embarked on campaigns to help those less able but, as time had gone on and things had become more serious, the bulletins seemed more interested in how many people had either contracted the virus or died of it.

Good news didn't seem to be on their agenda anymore and concerned citizens reaching out to the helpless counted as good news it appeared.

Tessa walked up the two flights of steps to her door and unlocked it.

As she did she heard movement above her. Footsteps. Someone was coming down the stairs from above.

She turned and looked up and saw Peter from the flat above descending.

For some reason he was dressed in just a pair of jogging bottoms. No shirt. No socks. Tessa was a little ashamed with herself for peering more closely than she should have at his very well developed torso and muscular arms. She knew, from their brief chats, that he'd been keen on visiting the gym and exactly how keen was now on view for her to see and enjoy.

She just about managed to suppress a smile, surprised at how quickly her thoughts had turned to more carnal matters just at the sight of Peter shirtless. That was what three months of lockdown did for you, she told herself.

'I saw you coming down the road,' he told her, not advancing any further down the stairs. 'Is everything all right?'

'I needed some stuff from the supermarket,' Tessa informed him.

'Oh, okay,' Peter went on. 'Claire and I wondered if you were all right. We're having a day to ourselves today. Not working from home. We're both sick of that. We thought we'd fill our time with something more pleasurable.' He grinned and Tessa understood why he was only half dressed.

The thought that the neighbours above her were filling their time by fucking each other's brains out, did nothing to lighten her mood but did quite a lot to make her feel that she was missing out.

'You lose track of time, shut in like this,' he offered.

Tessa nodded.

'I hate it,' she admitted. 'It makes you realise what animals in a zoo feel like. I just want to get back to normal. I'm sure everyone else does too. I haven't seen my parents for six months.'

'Are they local?'

'No but even if I had a car I'd be scared of visiting them in case I put them at risk.'

'We're all at risk, Tess,' he said, mournfully. 'This isn't just something old people and pregnant women have to be scared of anymore. We're all in danger.'

'Do you believe that?' she wanted to know.

'It's what the experts seem to think.'

'Are there any experts on this? I'm beginning to wonder.'

'Best just do as we're told, eh?'

'Isn't that what the Nazi's used to say?'

They both laughed. The sound echoing up and down the stairwell. It was a long time since such a joyous noise had been heard in the building but it died away rapidly.

'We just wondered if you wanted anything,' he announced.

'Just an end to all this,' Tessa said, wearily. 'But I don't think that's likely to happen any time soon. Do you?'

Peter sucked in a breath.

'Unfortunately no,' he murmured, still half way up the stairs. 'I'm socially distancing,' he chuckled, indicating the space between them.

'You and Claire obviously aren't?' Tessa grinned.

Peter smiled more broadly.

'We'll try not to disturb you,' he said, cheerfully. 'She's a bit of an animal when she gets going though.' He smiled again.

'That's good for you,' Tessa chuckled. 'But I don't mind. You enjoy yourselves.'

Peter raised his eyebrows. 'Don't worry, we will. You look after yourself.'

He turned and prepared to walk back up the stairs and Tessa found her gaze lingering just a little too long on his back and buttocks. She administered a swift mental rebuke and then pushed open her door.

It was dark and gloomy in the small hallway and Tessa snapped on the light, wanting to banish the blackness. She made her way through to the sitting room and put the TV on immediately. Even if they were just pedalling more depressing news about the virus. Even if it was just yet another re-run of a quiz show or some Reality

TV garbage at least it was company for her. Other voices to drown out those inside her head. The sound of the television was better than the silence inside the flat. She didn't like being alone with her own thoughts for too long.

She decided to make a cup of tea, not sure whether or not to listen as the newsreader droned on about more deaths, more government sanctions to combat the virus (mostly concerned with keeping people away from each other) and the desperate need for a cure.

Tessa glanced up at her ceiling and tried not to think too hard about Peter and Claire and what they were getting up to. Although the thoughts were rather pleasing if she was honest. There were worse things she could occupy her mind with.

While she waited for the kettle to boil she put the meagre supply of shopping away then wandered through into the first of the bedrooms to change. She took off her jeans and socks and slipped on a pair of leggings, content to pad around the flat barefoot for the rest of the day. After all, she wasn't going out again was she? Why not relax?

And do what?

Sit gazing blankly at the TV? Go online and read the latest developments there? Read? Do a jigsaw?

She had friends she could message. Friends she could Facetime with. But what the hell would she talk to them about? It wasn't as if she particularly wanted to share her exciting trip to the supermarket with them. Tessa shook her head and actually managed to smile thinly.

As she headed back towards the living room she paused beside the door of her second bedroom.

She barely went in there. It was stuffed with things she hadn't unpacked since she moved in. The detritus of a life. She couldn't face that now.

She heard movement on the stairs beyond her door and wondered if Peter had come down for something else. Perhaps he had come down to invite her upstairs to join himself and Claire. Tessa grinned at her aberrant thoughts. But those thoughts were rather pleasing if she was honest. She felt a tingle run through her.

Dirty bitch. Go and make your tea.

She was still smiling when she heard the knock on the door.

15.

The smile spread more widely across Tessa's face as she moved towards the door.

Was that Peter? Was he standing there now waiting for her to open up so he could ask her if she wanted to join him and Claire upstairs? Tessa shook her head, trying to dismiss the thought.

What the hell is wrong with you? Your mind is working overtime. That kind of thing only happened in porn videos.

She was still trying to force the thought from her mind as she reached for the lock, turning it and pulling the door open.

'Okay then, if you want me to join you...' she began but the sentence faded away rapidly.

So did her smile.

She had no idea who the young man facing her was.

Chris Whiteman smiled and nodded, trying to hold her gaze but looking her up and down from her face to her bare feet.

'Hello,' he said.

'Er…hello,' Tessa replied, completely taken aback by the newcomer. She wondered if he might have recently moved into the block of flats. It wasn't unusual for someone new to move in and for the other residents to not even catch sight of them unless their paths crossed in the hallways, on the stairs or down by the mail boxes. Was this where this young man had come from?

She felt suddenly exposed beneath his gaze and she stepped behind the half

open door a little more as if anxious to hide her shapely body from his sight.

'Can I help you?' she said, her voice faltering a little.

Whiteman brought one hand out from behind his back and held up pack of cigarettes, brandishing them as if he were presenting her with the Holy Grail.

Tessa looked puzzled.

'You…you…dropped these,' Whiteman said. 'On the path back there.' He motioned over his shoulder.

Tessa frowned.

'I don't think I did,' she said.

'Yeah, they…er…fell out of your shopping bag. I saw them. I was walking behind you. I'm going to my mate's house. I saw you and I saw your fags fall out of your bag.' He laughed awkwardly.

Tessa hesitated, glancing from the young man's face to the packet of cigarettes he was still holding.

'They're not mine,' she went on. 'You keep them.'

'Just trying to be a bit public spirited,' he laughed. 'You have to help each other in these times don't you?'

Tessa nodded slowly.

'You say you were going to see your mate?' she murmured.

'Yeah, he...he lives round the corner from here. That's why I was walking this way.'

'What about social distancing?'

'What the fuck?'

'Well, we're all supposed to be keeping away from other people aren't we? You might catch something from your mate. Or he might give you something.'

'What do you mean? This fucking virus?'

Tessa nodded.

'I don't believe what they're saying,' Whiteman went on. 'I think it's bullshit. I don't think this virus is as serious as they say.'

'Well, thousands have died of it,' she reminded him. 'Thousands more will if we don't do as the government say.'

'Fuck the government,' snapped Whiteman.

Tessa was surprised at the venom in his tone. She took a step back, pushing the door a couple of inches, wanting it closed, wanting this interloper to go.

'I mean, they don't know what's going on really, do they?" Whiteman went on, trying to control the anger in his voice. "They don't know nothing about how people have to live. Not real people. They only know about rich cunts, like themselves.'

Tessa held his gaze for a second. His eyes were blazing as he spoke. Each word tinged with anger now.

'Excuse my language,' he grunted. 'Sorry. But I mean, this virus, it's only killing old people, isn't it?'

'At the moment,' Tessa reminded him. 'If we don't do as we're told, it could get worse.'

'Yeah, right,' Whiteman said, dismissively. 'Anyway, you going to take your fags?'

'I told you, they're not mine.'

'But I saw you drop them.'

'You couldn't have. And would you mind telling me how you got into these flats? They're private you know.'

'The main door was open. I just walked in. I wanted to find you so I could give you these.' Again he held up the pack of cigarettes.

'They're not mine, thanks anyway,' Tessa told him, pushing the door slightly.

'They are,' Whiteman snapped, putting up one hand, resting his palm against the door she had tried to close on him.

'Can you take your hand away please?' Tessa said, her voice catching. She felt suddenly afraid. He looked at her unblinkingly and she could see something behind his eyes that she didn't care for.

'You should try being a bit more grateful,' Whiteman rasped, pushing against the door.

'Please just go,' Tessa muttered.

'Fucking bitch,' snarled Whiteman and he suddenly threw all his weight against the door.

It swung back hard, slamming into Tessa, knocking her off her feet.

She tried to scream but all that came forth was a gasp of terror. She fell backwards against the wall behind her, banging her head so hard she felt dizzy. To her horror she realised that not only was she losing consciousness but that Whiteman was forcing his way in, stepping across the threshold until he towered above her.

'Please,' Tessa moaned, darkness closing in around her.

She saw Whiteman smiling down at her, his breath coming in short gasps.

She felt sick. Her head spinning.

Whiteman stepped nearer.

Tessa raised both hands to ward him off but it was useless.

She blacked out.

16.

It felt as if someone was inside her head trying to drill their way out.

Tessa opened her eyes slightly then closed them rapidly as if that simple act might make the pain go away.

It didn't.

At first she wasn't sure where she was. She remembered falling, remembered slamming her head against the wall. Remembered the man crashing into her flat and...

Oh God. Where was he?

She lifted her head, sharp pain filling her skull.

It took her a second to realise she was lying on her sofa. How the hell did she get in here? How...

'Are you feeling better?'

The voice came from behind her. From the kitchen area of the flat. The small dwelling was divided into two bedrooms, a bathroom, a tiny hallway and a kitchen/living area divided by a breakfast bar. It was from the area near the cooker that the voice came.

Tessa tried to sit up but the pain in her head prevented that simple action and she sank back onto the cushions beneath her, groaning softly.

'You fell over,' the voice went on. 'You banged your head.'

Tessa realised that the voice belonged to Whiteman and that realisation sent a cold shiver through her. He was inside her flat. He was only feet from her. She lay still, her eyes closed.

'Please,' she said, softly. 'Please don't hurt me.'

Silence greeted her words but instead she heard a floorboard creak as Whiteman moved across the room towards her.

'I made you a cup of tea,' he said. 'I thought it might make you feel better.'

She swallowed hard and turned her head slightly to see that Whiteman was standing beside the sofa. As she watched he lowered himself into the armchair next to her, a mug of tea cradled in his hands.

'You fell over and knocked yourself out,' he said. 'I brought you in here. I thought you should lay down.'

'Please don't hurt me,' Tessa said. 'Just take what you want and go.'

Whiteman didn't speak.

'I haven't got much money but my purse is over there in my handbag and…'

'I don't want your money,' he snapped.

'I've got food in the cupboards. I know how valuable that is now. Take it. Please. Take what you want but just don't hurt me.'

'You think I broke in here to nick your food?'

She looked blankly at him.

'You wouldn't be the first person to steal food since this lockdown started,' she reminded him.

'People are scared. Scared people do bad things.'

'Like you?' she said, defiantly.

Whiteman smiled thinly and pushed the mug of tea towards her.

'Drink this,' he said. 'It'll make you feel better.'

Tessa looked at the mug then at Whiteman.

'I haven't put poison in it,' he told her, grinning.

Tessa sat up slightly, relieved that her head didn't feel any worse. She took the mug from him, raised it to her lips and sipped.

'How do you feel?' he wanted to know.

'I'd feel better if you'd go,' Tessa said.

'Girls like you are all the same,' he grunted. 'Good looking girls. You think you can treat people like shit and get away with it just because you're fucking fit.'

'I don't know you. I've never been horrible to you. I haven't treated you like shit. I don't even know you.'

Whiteman looked at her, his gaze running slowly from her bare feet to her slender legs.

Tessa sucked in a breath as she saw him pull at his groin as he gazed at her.

'You got a boyfriend?' he asked, his voice low.

'That's none of your business,' she said, trying to inject some strength into her voice.

'I bet you have,' Whiteman told her. 'Girls like you always have boyfriends. Guys always go for girls like you. What does he do? Is he in IT or something like that?' He grinned.

'I told you, it's none of your business.'

'Go on, tell me. Talk to me. With all this lockdown and self-isolating bullshit people haven't spoken to anyone for ages. They might not talk to them again face to face for fuck knows how long. I thought you might like a little chat.' Again he grinned but there was no humour in the gesture.

Tessa took another sip of the tea, wondering how she should play this. Should she go along with him? Try to placate him until she found out what he really wanted?

It's pretty obvious what he wants. He doesn't want your money or your food. What else have you got that he might want? How about what's between your legs?

Tessa tried to swallow but her throat was dry despite the tea she was drinking.

She took another sip.

'Look, we can talk if you want,' she told him, quietly. 'You're right. Since this started we've all forgotten how to talk to each other. How to be friendly.'

Whiteman nodded slowly.

'I agree with you,' Tessa went on, her tone as placatory as she could make it.

'What about you? How are you coping with what's happening?'

Whiteman looked more intently at her.

'Do you really care or are you just trying to make me drop my guard'' he said, flatly.

'I want to talk,' Tessa went on.

'Really?'

'Why not? Like you say, no one's spoken to each other face to face for months. You can't count Skype and Face-time can you?' She managed to smile and was relieved when Whiteman smiled too.

'I suppose we should be sitting more than two metres away from each other,' he said. 'That's the distance you're supposed to be isn't it?'

'Unless they've made it more since this morning,' Tessa said. 'I put the news on most mornings but it's just so depressing hearing the same stuff over and over again. Death tolls. How overworked the NHS is. How many more have got it.'

'You need something to take your mind off it all,' Whiteman told her, still pulling at his groin.

Tessa tried not to look. She sipped more tea and sat up a little more.

'So,' Whiteman breathed. 'Tell me about your boyfriend. When was the last time you and him fucked?'

As he spoke, he started to unzip his jeans.

17.

Adam stayed in the car as per their demand. They had taken the car key from the ignition so he couldn't get any funny ideas and drive off. Sharon remained in the back. Just as the others had a knife, so had she.

Adam was watching the three lads as they approached the house. It was Kevin's idea to come to this place and so he was the one to knock the door.

'Why are you doing this?' Adam didn't bother turning to speak to the girl. With only the two of them in earshot, it was obvious who he was talking to. Sharon didn't bother to answer him, not that he really expected her to.

There was a scream from outside as an elderly woman opened a door only to get pushed back inside. Adam watched. Billy was last through the door. He slammed it shut. It really was just the two of them now; Adam and Sharon. If only they had left the car key. He would have started the engine up and driven head first into a wall with a hope of catapulting the bitch from the back seat, out the windscreen.

'You know you won't get away with any of this, right?' Adam glanced into the rear-view mirror. Sharon wasn't even looking at him. She was staring in the direction of the house. He wasn't sure but he thought there could have been a genuine look of concern in her eyes.

'Does it really matter anymore what any of us do?' Sharon startled Adam with her response. He'd presumed she would have stayed quiet for the duration.

'What do you mean?'

'This virus. The way the world is going. Borders shut down. Stores being run with limitations. People too scared to leave. Jobs being lost. Debt levels rising... What does any of it matter anymore?'

The way she spoke surprised Adam. There was a certain level of articulation there that he hadn't expected given how he'd heard the others speak; stuttering, garbled sentences with more swearing than entirely necessary. Here, she almost sounded educated. *Almost*.

'Fuck them. People bring all this about themselves and - the way things are going - we might as well enjoy the last moments of freedom we have.' She paused a moment before adding, 'We'll probably be all dead within a month anyway the way the virus is spreading.'

Adam didn't say anything. What was there to say? The fact they'd all most likely be dead soon was probably right with the way the world was going and how little the government really seemed to be doing. And if the world was to continue like this, maybe death would be better?

'The world won't ever be the same again,' she added. 'Now we just need to make our mark so that, when the dust settles, we're the ones standing on top.'

Again, there was sense to what she was saying. There was no sense to what they were doing in the house though, or what they'd done to Dave and Anett.

'Who lives here?' Adam wasn't really sure if he wanted the answer to his question. In truth, he hadn't meant to ask it. It just slipped out to save the silence. To his relief, Sharon didn't answer. She only smiled. Unbeknownst to her, Adam breathed a heavy sigh of relief. He didn't need to know who lived there and nor did he need to know what they were doing.

Adam glanced back to the woman in the rear. She wasn't the biggest of people. Had it not been for the knife, he would have easily overpowered her. It was the thought at the forefront of his mind now. If he was going to try anything to get away, now was the time. His mind cast back to what they'd been looking at on the phone. More important, *her* reaction to it. She had been disgusted. Then there was the fact she hadn't gone into the house with them… Whatever they were doing in there, it wouldn't have been good and yet, she wanted no part of it and opted to stay with Adam instead.

'You're not like them,' he said as he scanned what was around the car. Bushes, trees… Plenty of places to hide from them once he left his car.

Sharon didn't say anything. She was still staring towards the house, wondering what they were doing in there.

'Yeah…' Adam paused a moment as he ran through his options once more. He continued, 'I'm not going to hang around for this.'

Before Sharon had a chance to respond, Adam flung his door open and climbed from the vehicle. He didn't bother closing the door behind him, he just started to head off towards the thickets.

Sharon jumped out of the back and called out, 'Don't fucking move...'

Adam ignored her. Instead, he continued walking. He just kept telling himself over and over that she wasn't like them. She was just pulled along for the ride and, even then, she probably didn't want to be there.

'I said, don't fucking move!'

When he ignored her again, Sharon ran towards Adam with the knife gripped tight in her hand. Hearing her footsteps behind, he spun on the spot to face her.

'Stay the fuck back...'

It was clear from the way she held the knife, Sharon had no idea what she was doing with it. When close enough, Adam moved fast to grab her wrist and, another quick movement, he snapped it back. The bone splintered under the skin and Sharon screamed in pain as she dropped the knife to the stoned-path. Adam grabbed it with his spare hand and, quick as a flash, thrust the blade into her throat cutting not just her vocal cord but the scream too. Shocked by his own actions, Adam released the knife and Sharon's broken wrist. He watched, in horror, as she stumbled back with eyes wide and a look of pure panic on her face.

'I'm sorry...' He didn't know why he felt the need to apologise. If it wasn't her, it would have been him with the knife jutting from his body.

Sharon staggered there a moment, gasping for breath that wouldn't come. Adam paused a moment before extending a hand towards her; a futile offer of help that wasn't meant. She didn't take his hand. She dropped to the ground in a seated position. Slowly, with a shaking hand, she pulled the knife from her throat. A jettison of blood splattered the stones before her and almost hit Adam's legs. He instinctively took a step back but it didn't stop there. He took another step, and another, and another and... He turned and started to run for the thicket. The thought in his head, *Just get away.*

*

Unaware what had happened outside, Kevin smiled at the old woman.

'What do you want?' The old woman looked at him with hatred burning in her eyes.

Kevin laughed at her brave hostility, as did his friends. Slowly, the smile faded from his face.

'Hello, mum,' he said. 'It's been a while.'

18.

On the other side of the thicket, out of sight of the house, Adam froze as he patted down his front pockets. His heart raced as he looked back towards where he'd left the car and - more importantly - his phone.

'Fuck, fuck, fuck, *fuck*!' There was a part of him that thought about going back to get it; a small, quiet little voice in his head saying he couldn't just leave the occupants in the house with *them*. The voice told him to get the phone, call the cops and then just fucking run. Get away from there as fast as possible but happy in the knowledge that help would be on its way. But there was another voice too; a louder one. *Just fucking run.*

Adam didn't know how long they were going to be inside for. For all he knew, they were already finished with whatever they were doing and were already on their way back to the car. Once they saw what he had done to their friend, there was no way he was getting away and doubted that whatever they would do to him would be quick, or pleasant.

That voice again: *Just fucking run.*

Adam faced forward. Trees and green all around him in an area he didn't know too well. The only thing he *did* know was that he couldn't go back the same way he came in. Not whilst they had the car keys *and* his fucking car. It would be easy for them to catch up. All he could do was pick a direction and hope that he would find someone who could help. So now the only question that remained was, left or right?

Adam hurried off to his right; the side with the most cover. Hopefully there'd be an old farmhouse, or something, tucked away behind some of it. A place where he could get to a phone at least and call for help; explain what had happened and what he'd been forced to do.

More panic set in as that little voice in his head kept telling him that he would be going to prison for this. No one would believe it was self-defence. They would just blame him and then, to make an example in these tough times, they would throw the book at him and send him down for the rest of his life.

Adam tried to push the thoughts from his head. *Now isn't the time.* The voice continued: *And they'd probably* *blame you for whatever is happening in the house too. Somehow they will blame it <u>all</u> on you.* His brain switched tact and asked: *What even is happening in the house?*

19.

BEFORE

Kevin was standing in the doorway to the living room. Sharon was a few feet behind. Their mother, Angela, was standing by the fireplace. The fire itself was roaring, warming up the coldness of the night. Angela's eyes were red from crying but, now, there was no hint of sadness on her expression, or in her tone. There was only the sound of bitter disappointment in her voice.

'You can't say I haven't done everything for you since your father left. I've made sure you have clean clothes, food in the cupboard... *Everything*. Did I ever ask you for anything? No. Did I say anything when you shouted at me for whatever reason? Taking your pathetic little mood swings out on me? No. I took it all; everything you could throw at me and yet I still loved you.' She stopped talking.

Kevin said nothing. He just stood there with his glaring eyes fixed to her. His jaw clenched as he stopped himself from saying anything. Behind him, Sharon was struggling to hold back the tears.

The pair had been arrested for shoplifting and Angela had had to go out and collect them from the station. She knew it was Kevin's idea and Sharon was just following his lead but she didn't care; she was mad at them both. Their antisocial behaviour was an ongoing issue and one Angela was struggling to control. The more she tried, the more they fought back and the nastier they got. Well, today… *Enough was enough.*

'Just get out.'

'What?'

'You heard me. I've had enough. I'm done. Get out.'

Kevin laughed. 'Whatever.' He turned to Sharon and said, 'Come on, let's go upstairs.'

Angela called out, 'No. Get out of the house. You think you're the big man? You think you know the way the world works and can get by in it? Fine. Get out of my house. Go. Make your own way.'

'You're kicking us out?'

Angela said nothing. She just turned her back on her children. *Her children?* These weren't her children anymore. They hadn't been for a number of years now, since *he* had left.

'And where are we supposed to go?'

Angela said nothing.

'I said where the fuck are we supposed to go?'

Angela snapped, 'Maybe you should have given that some thought before you kept throwing everything back in my face? You want to go around living by your own rules and doing what you want? Fine, you can. But it won't be under my roof and I won't be there to support you anymore.' She added, 'Either of you!'

Kevin hesitated a moment as his brain raced with various ways of handling this situation. Apologise? Beg? Say he would change? Or - as usual - go off the deep end… 'Fine. Fuck you. Fuck your house. Fuck everything about you. We don't need you. You're a pathetic, weak woman and that's why you lost dad and, now, why you lost us. So, yeah, fuck you.'

'GET OUT!'

*

NOW

'What do you want?'

'Just checking in on you, mum.' Kevin smiled. 'It has been a while since we talked and things have changed and, well, I was worried about you…'

'You were worried about me?'

Kevin laughed.

'Is that so hard to believe?'

'You don't care about anyone but yourself.' Angela added, 'I don't know what twisted you so much but you're not the loving child I raised.'

'No. I'm not. A survivalist, unlike you. You just rolled over when dad left. He walked out on you and you rolled over and played dead and yet you said I was the weak one.' He laughed again and then shook his head. 'I'm not here to talk about this though. I'm here to check up on you.'

Angela didn't say anything. Instead, she waited for the punch-line. She had known Kevin long enough to know there'd be one coming.

'Are you staying isolated as per the guidelines for people over a certain age?' Kevin raised an eyebrow.

She said nothing.

'You are, aren't you? You always did like to live by the rules. But this is what was worrying me... I was worried you'd be locked away, waiting for this to all blow-over.'

'That worried you?'

Kevin nodded.

'It did. If you're locking yourself away from people... How are you going to get this virus and just fucking die.'

Angela couldn't hide the tears forming in her eyes.

'Because that's what Sharon and I want from you now. We want you to die.' He smiled at his mother again as a single tear rolled down her cheek.

'I regret the day you were born.'

Kevin laughed.

'One day, that might have hurt me. But - today - we are in agreement. I regret being born too. At least, to a mother like you. Anyway, I'm not here to chat... I'm just here to make sure you do as Sharon and I want.' He turned to Darren and nodded to him. Darren knew what he wanted and pulled the knife from where he'd earlier hidden it under his top. He passed it to Kevin.

'What are you doing?' Angela asked as she took a step back.

'I'm doing the world a favour.'

Kevin slowly walked closer to Angela. She made no effort to back up from him.

'I hope one day you realise what you've become and that it eats at you.'

Kevin smiled wider. 'I won't ever regret this.'

He put a tender hand on his mother's shoulder and gave it a little squeeze as he winked at her. She tried to show no emotion but failed as her bottom lip quivered. Billy and Darren were grinning now too.

'Do it,' Darren said.

Billy reached for his phone and started to film as - slowly - Kevin pushed the blade into Angela's stomach. She gasped in response as her son pulled her closer to him. The blade was all but gone. Only the handle was visible.

'We won't grieve for you.'

Kevin slowly twisted the blade around in his mother's gut as she fell against him. He kept her standing there with his other hand still on her shoulder.

He said again, 'We won't grieve for you.'

Kevin pushed his mother back and she slumped to the floor. He watched as she struggled to cling to life. Billy stepped forward and put the camera in her face in order to get the last few moments of her existence captured through the view-finder.

Kevin didn't mind. He just asked, 'Send me a copy of that?'

'Sure.'

'Such a pretty mouth for an old cunt,' Billy said. 'Should have got her to suck my dick before you stabbed her.'

'Dude… That's my mum.'

The three of them laughed. Angela's final breath exhaled slowly from between her lips. Billy stopped recording.

20

"Please don't" Tessa said, her voice faltering.

Whiteman eased his zip down further, a growing smile on his face.

'I'm not going to hurt you,' he told her, his voice low, barely above a whisper. 'You wanted to talk didn't you? Well, so do I.' He unbuttoned his jeans, easing them down slightly his gaze never leaving Tessa's face.

She shrank back slightly, pushing herself against the sofa as if she hoped she could disappear into the material.

Whiteman pulled up his top slightly and she caught sight of bare flesh.

'You want to talk?' she murmured. 'What do you want to talk about?' Tessa had trouble controlling her breathing now.

'I want to know about you,' Whiteman said. 'I want to find out things about you.' Again he smiled.

'What kind of things?' Tessa asked, her voice barely more than a whisper.

'Well, you're a pretty girl. You can tell me about your boyfriend. Tell me about what you and he get up to. What do you like? What does he do to you?'

Tessa was shaking now.

Whiteman eased his jeans and pants down a few more inches and a very hard penis sprang into view. He closed his fingers around it and started gently rubbing it.

'When did you last get fucked?' he wanted to know.

'I haven't got a boyfriend,' Tessa insisted.

'Bollocks,' he sneered.

'I haven't. I'm telling you the truth. I don't know what you want me to say.'

'I want you to tell me the truth. If you haven't got a boyfriend you must play with yourself, right?' His hand began to move a little quicker on his erection. 'When did you do that last? Today? Yesterday? Tell me what you did. You got a vibrator? I bet you fucking have.'

Tessa felt sick. She sucked in a deep breath, trying not to look at Whiteman who was now rubbing his penis more rhythmically.

'Stand up,' he said. 'I want to look at you.'

She propped the mug of tea on the arm of the sofa and got to her feet, her knees almost buckling.

'Please don't do this,' she breathed. 'Please.' She was fighting back tears now.

Whiteman grunted and Tessa closed her eyes.

'Look what you've done to me,' he groaned. 'Look.'

She kept her eyes tightly shut.

'I told you to look,' he insisted, his voice rising in volume slightly. 'Look at me.'

Tessa reluctantly did as he asked, trying to keep her eyes fixed on his. He was still rubbing his stiff shaft, pushing his hips towards her.

'Look how hard you got me,' he sighed, still moving his hand up and down his erection. 'You dirty fucking bitch.' He laughed and it raised the hairs on the back of her neck. 'Look at my cock. Look at it.'

She closed her eyes.

'Fucking look at it, you cunt.'

The words were roared at her. They reverberated inside the small room and Tessa shuddered as he bellowed.

For a brief second she wondered if someone else in the block might have heard. They might have heard the words and already be coming to help her. There would be a knock on the door any second, someone calling her to ask if she was okay. Asking if she needed help. She would run to the door and let her rescuers in and that would be the end of this intruder. Police would drag him away. She would give evidence against him in court. He'd be locked up and...

'Take off your leggings.'

When Whiteman spoke again his voice had returned to a low, menacing whisper. She looked at him and saw that he'd pulled a mobile phone from his pocket. He was holding it up, capturing her image.

The sick fucker was taking pictures.

She heard the click.

And again.

Whiteman chuckled.

'Wait until they see you,' he grunted.

'Who?' Tessa wanted to know.

'I'm sending these to my friends,' he told her. 'They'll like them.'

Tessa clenched her fists, her terror turning rapidly to anger.

'Now take the leggings off,' he repeated, still holding up the phone. 'You want to look good on video don't you?'

Without opening her eyes and shaking so violently she could barely grip the material, she dug her thumbs into the top of her leggings and began to pull them down.

'No, no, no,' Whiteman chided. 'Do it slowly. Do it like you do when you undress for your boyfriend. Make it sexy.' Again, he laughed. Again, she felt the hairs on the back of her neck rise.

Tessa did as he instructed, pulling her leggings down over her slim hips, to her thighs and then to her knees.

'Oh, yeah,' Whiteman grunted, putting the phone down and Tessa glanced at him long enough to see that he was masturbating faster now. 'Go on, you fucking bitch. Take them right off.'

She did as he asked, kicking them free. She stood there in just her t-shirt and knickers, listening to his laboured breathing as he drew nearer his climax.

Once it's over he might go. Just let him do what he wants to do. Get him out. No matter what you have to do.

'Sit down and stretch your legs out in front of you,' Whiteman demanded, moving a little closer now, his hand still moving rapidly on his shaft. 'You've got fucking great legs. Open them a bit.' He reached for the phone with his free hand, snapping off some more photos.

Tessa did as he told her. He moved forward again. He was only three or four feet from her now.

'Oh fuck, yeah,' he moaned, his gaze fixed on her thighs, his pleasure almost total. 'Take off your knickers.'

This time she could not hold back the tears. She sat motionless for a moment, her body shaking slightly, her eyes filling. Tears began to course down her cheeks.

'Take them off,' he grunted.

She hesitated a moment longer.

'I'll fucking kill you if you don't,' he assured her, his voice thick and mucoid now.

'There are other things I can do for you,' she whimpered, her face contorted, her cheeks glistening with tears.

Whiteman gasped then suddenly squeezed his penis hard and grunted.

'I know. That's why I'm not going to shoot my fucking load yet,' he breathed. 'Why do it now when I can shoot it in your mouth? Or your cunt? Or your arse? Or all over your fucking face.' He grinned. 'You'd love that wouldn't you? Tell me you want me to do that. Tell me you want me to fucking use you. Tell me.'

She nodded.

'Tell me,' he persisted. 'Tell me. I want to hear you say it. Tell me you want to suck my cock.' His voice rose suddenly in volume once again. 'Fucking tell me.'

21

Tessa barely thought about what she was doing.

It was a purely instinctive reaction.

A survival instinct?

She grabbed the mug of tea that was still on the arm of the sofa and hurled the hot liquid at Whiteman.

Most of it hit its target. The hot brown fluid splashed over his stomach and genitals and he shouted in pain.

Tessa found herself wishing that the tea had been boiling. She wanted him to feel *real* pain. She wanted him in agony.

Whiteman was more startled than hurt by the fact that the hot tea had showered his penis. On the bulbous tip of his erection it was more painful and he yelped as he felt pain spreading through his lower body.

'Fucking bitch,' he hissed, backing away.

Tessa jumped to her feet, swinging one foot upwards with tremendous power. Her instep connected with his groin with a satisfyingly hard impact. She saw him grimace, heard him shout in pain and surprise. A s   h e stumbled backwards she kicked out at him again, this time driving her heel into his left kneecap. She was certainly no martial arts expert and she'd never been in a fight in her life but, more by luck than judgement and with a strength born of desperation, she managed to hurt him. He dropped to the ground, clutching at his knee, his jeans still around his thighs.

He looked faintly ridiculous and, if the situation had been different she might have laughed but, she knew she had to move quickly while he was struggling.

She kicked at him again but, this time, he managed to grab her ankle and he held her for a second, Tessa balancing unsteadily on one foot.

Whiteman jerked his hands up hard and she toppled backwards, tumbling over the arm of the sofa.

She hit the floor hard but rolled onto her stomach and then hauled herself up again, trying to reach the kitchen area, desperate to find something she could use as a weapon.

Whiteman, his jeans still around his thighs, threw himself at her, slamming into her and driving them both into the doors of the cupboards beneath a work top close to the sink.

One of the doors, loosened by the impact, swung open revealing the cleaning materials inside.

Tessa grabbed for the nearest object and closed her fingers around. The bottle of kitchen cleaner was a handy club and she struck out wildly with it, slamming it into Whiteman's temple with as much force as she could muster but it did little to halt his frenzied attack.

He was laying on top of her now and she could feel his penis pressing against her crotch as he struggled against her. He grabbed a handful of her hair, tugging hard on it, several long hairs coming free. But Tessa barely felt the pain. It seemed to spur her on to greater effort and she managed to tilt the bleach bottle upwards, shoving the nozzle into his face again as she pressed the spray.

A stream of bleach squirted into Whiteman's face, some of it into his eyes.

He shrieked in pain and rolled off Tessa who dragged herself upright, kicking out at him, stamping on his chest. On his shoulders. On his face.

She split his bottom lip as he writhed in agony, clutching at his eyes.

The sight of his blood spurting from the gash in his lip drove her on. She had the upper hand now. She had to finish this.

There were a couple of saucepans on the drying rack next to the sink and Tessa snatched up the largest of them, gripping the handle with both hands as she brought it down on his head. She hit him once, twice. Three times. Hard, numbing blows that took all her strength.

Whiteman tried again to grab her but she struck him again. More powerful blows to his scalp and forehead the second of which opened a large cut just below his hairline.

She kept hitting him.

The cartoon clang of the metal saucepan against his cranium continued.

Tessa hit him across the nose and shattered it, more blood bursting from the ruined appendage.

Whiteman tried to roll over, to escape this rain of blows but he was becoming increasingly weak.

Why was he still conscious? In films when someone was hit on the head they dropped like a stone and didn't get up.

Tessa hit him again. And again.

Whiteman groaned, blood spilling over his lips but Tessa could barely hold the saucepan anymore. The handle was slick with crimson fluid but the sheer effort of hammering blows down upon her attacker had caused the strength in those blows to diminish.

The saucepan slipped from her grasp.

Tessa staggered back, her hand dragging open a draw. She reached in and managed to pull out a kitchen knife.

As she saw Whiteman clamber to his feet she stepped forward and drove the blade into his stomach.

When he toppled backwards the blade remained stuck fast and it was pulled from her hand. Blood exploded from the wound and Whiteman used both hands to grip the savage laceration. He dropped to his knees, his eyes rolling upwards in the sockets.

Tessa stood glaring at him for a moment, wondering why the blows with the saucepan hadn't knocked him out and yet now, the knife seemed to be robbing him of consciousness.

Whiteman slumped onto his side, eyes closed.

Tessa stood motionless for a moment, her terrified gaze never leaving the body before her. Then she moved towards him and prodded him with the toes of one foot, watching as he rolled onto his back, the knife still protruding from his stomach.

She wondered if he was dead but, as she looked more closely, she could see his chest rising and falling slowly.

Tessa didn't know whether to be happy or annoyed that he was still breathing.

Only now did she realise that his jeans were still around his thighs, his genitals exposed.

She stamped ferociously on his testicles and penis.

'You bastard,' she hissed, tears now beginning to flow freely.

Tears of relief? Of triumph?

It was a long time before she stopped crying.

22

The stairwell smelled of food.

Someone was cooking something in one of the other flats.

Peter Miller descended slowly, trying to figure out exactly what the aroma was that was floating on the air. Curry? Chilli? Something more exotic? Whatever it was it was making him feel hungry. After his exertions with Claire earlier in the day, he'd built up something of an appetite.

He smiled to himself as he thought back to their rampant carnality. If that was a way of passing time during self isolation then it wasn't all bad, he thought. They'd have to put aside a day every week of their isolation to indulge the way they had earlier.

As he reached the floor below he tried to push those thoughts from his mind.

That wasn't what he should be thinking of now. His descent from his own flat to this floor was spurred by more noble motives.

He and Claire had heard the banging and shouting below them about ninety minutes ago.

Raised voices.

One in particular that they didn't recognise.

Then a period of silence and then, more movement.

They had been unable to ignore the sounds from below them, distracted once or twice from their own antics by the noise. Once the cacophony had ended and their own passions were spent, they had discussed the noises and who might have made them. They had very obviously come from Tessa's flat.

Had she just had her TV on too loud? Was she in trouble? They had discussed every manner of possible solution for the barrage of noises but had not settled on a suitable explanation. Finally, they had decided that they should investigate or, more to the point, Claire had decided that Peter should investigate.

She said he only had to pop down and just check that everything was okay. He could explain why to Tessa if she asked.

Nevertheless, he felt a little awkward as he approached the door of Tessa's flat.

He stood there motionless for a moment then tapped lightly on the door.

There was no answer.

Peter waited and knocked again.

Still no sound from within.

He was about to knock for a third time when he wondered if it might be more sensible to call for the police?

Why? Just because someone hasn't answered their door? She might be out getting essential shopping or taking some exercise or something similarly innocuous. The police weren't going to be happy if they were summoned for something so trivial. They had more important things to do like ensuring not more than three people congregated in a field or making sure no one panic buying in a supermarket got within two metres of any other stock-piling shopper.

Peter took a deep breath and knocked again.

The door was opened immediately.

Tessa stood there smiling broadly.

'Hello, again,' she said, happily. 'We'll have to stop meeting like this.'

He smiled, a little unsure of how to word what he had to say.

'Taking a break from your fun day?' Tessa asked, grinning more broadly.

'You could say that,' Peter confessed. 'I...we...just wondered if you were all right.'

'I told you earlier I went to the shops and…'

He cut across her. 'No, I know that. I didn't mean all right for food. We thought we heard some noises earlier, from down here. We were worried.'

'What sort of noises?' Tessa enquired.

'Raised voices. Shouting. And some banging.'

Tessa chuckled.

'Sorry, I bought a new TV last week and it's the first time I've used it. I thought I'd better do something useful during self-isolation so I sorted it out. Put it in the living room and took the old one out. I'm not used to volume yet. Sorry.' She was surprised at how easily the lie came. 'Do you want to see it?' She stepped back, ushering him into the flat.

'Oh, no that's okay,' Peter protested. 'As long as you're all right. That was all that mattered.'

'Come in anyway,' Tessa insisted. 'We can have a cup of tea or something. As long as we stay two metres away from each other.'

'That's very kind of you,' Peter told her. 'But...'

'I won't take no for an answer,' Tessa went on. 'The kettle's just boiled. Come on.'

Peter nodded and stepped inside, barely able to stand in the tiny hallway beside Tessa without bumping into her.

'After you,' he said, watching as she took the couple of strides that took her to the sitting room door. She opened it and walked in. Peter followed her into the room.

Tessa motioned to the sofa and he seated himself on the end of it, looking around.

It was a well kept flat. Nicely decorated and with a healthy selection of house plants and flowers dotted around in vases and containers. There was a bookshelf against the far wall, crowded with hardbacks and paper-backs. There were more shelves supporting hundreds of DVDs and the entire room was dominated by a large television that was currently showing a news bulletin.

Peter glanced at the screen, reading the latest Corona Virus news as it ran below the newsreader like some kind of electronic ticker-tape.

'I wonder when it's ever going to end,' Tessa said, pouring boiling water onto a couple of teabags.

'God knows,' Peter shrugged. 'When it started I was a bit cynical but, the longer its gone on I've stopped being cynical and got scared instead.' He took the mug of tea from her and sipped it.

'No one seems to talk about anything else anymore. It's all over the news. Even when I message friends all they want to talk about is the bloody virus. How it's affecting them. If they know anyone who's got it. That kind of thing.'

'It does make you wonder if things will ever get back to normal.'

'Whatever normal is.'

They both laughed.

'I'm quite looking forward to getting back to work,' he confessed. 'It's okay being at home but I like the routine of going out, travelling and walking into an office.'

'I know what you mean. Working from home takes far too much discipline.'

They laughed once more.

'I wish I had a garden at a time like this,' Tessa went on. 'I'd love to potter about.'

'You like a potter do you?' Peter said, smiling.

'I do,' Tessa grinned. 'And I'd like to be able to hang washing out on a sunny day instead of draping it over the furniture waiting for it to dry.'

He nodded and glanced at his watch.

'I'd better go,' Peter murmured. 'Claire will be wondering what's happened to me.'

'Well, thank her for her concern, both of you, but I'm fine and please apologise to her from me for the noise.'

Peter got to his feet and Tessa walked behind him to the door. They exchanged a few more words at the threshold and then he turned and made his way back up the stairs, waving happily. Tessa waited a moment then closed the door, turning the key in the lock.

She let out a long breath and swallowed, relieved that he'd left.

23

Kevin's scream echoed across the English countryside. He dropped the bloody knife to the ground and hurried over to where Sharon was lying on her back. He fell to his knees and scooped her limp body up in his arms and out of the pool of blood that had collected beneath her. Tears of anger and grief ran down his cheeks as he cradled her close.

Billy and Darren looked all around for signs of Adam.

'Where the fuck did he go?'

'I can't see him…'

'We can't let him get away…'

'It wasn't my idea to fucking take the cunt hostage.'

'But you didn't argue it at the fucking time, did you?'

'Fuck you. This isn't my fault.'

Kevin shouted at them both, 'Shut the fuck up! Will you both just shut the fuck up! I told you not fucking leave her in the car with him! I fucking told you!'

Darren snapped back, 'And she had a fucking knife! She could have protected herself if she wanted to and…'

Kevin laid his dead sister back down on the ground and sprung up to his feet. 'And what?'

Billy stepped between them in an effort to try and act as peace-keeper.

'And she was too weak to help herself, you cunt.'

Kevin lunged at Darren only to be stopped by Billy. Sensibly, Darren took a step back.

'She could have come with us,' Darren said. 'We could have forced that fuck to come with us too had she wanted to. We could have all stayed together but, no… She refused because she was a fucking coward and now, because of that, she paid the ultimate price and if we don't find that cunt, we'll end up in prison so quit acting like a fucking bitch, accept it and let's go and find that son of a bitch.'

Kevin broke down. Billy just held him, unsure of what he could say that would make any of this better. In truth: There were no words.

'All the time we're standing here, he is getting away from us,' Darren said coldly. 'You want that little prick? We need to go now!'

'Where exactly?' Kevin said, fighting back the tears. 'Where in the fuck are we meant to find him? He could have gone anywhere.'

The three of them stood there, looking all around once more. He really could have gone anywhere.

'We need to split up,' Billy said. He released Kevin from his grip and reached into his pocket for Adam's car key. 'I'll take the car back down the road. You two... I suggest one fuck heads that way,' he said with a point, 'and the other in the opposite direction. Take it you all got phones? We find him, we send a message to warn the others.'

'Needle in a fucking haystack,' Darren said as he looked up and down the area once more.

'So what? You want to stand here and moan like a cunt? Better to look and not find him than stay here and just wait for the fucking pigs to come for us, right? Jesus fucking Christ. I got to remind you, this was your idea?'

'My idea? It wasn't my idea for mummy's boy to visit his bitch-arse mother.'

'But it was your idea to fucking come out here and do whatever the fuck we wanted...'

'Because you put up much or an argument?'

'WE'RE WASTING TIME!' Kevin grabbed the knife from the ground and marched off towards the tree-line. He called back, 'You fucks find him… You keep him alive for me. He's mine!'

Billy and Darren watched him for a moment before Darren shrugged and said, 'Guess I'll head that way.'

'Yeah well just fucking message each other if we find him.'

'*If,*' Darren reiterated.

'Just fucking look for him, for fuck sake.' Billy turned and started towards the car. There, he opened the door and jumped into the driver's seat before sliding the key into the ignition.

He looked to the gear-stick and went to select first, only to stop when he noticed a mobile phone sitting there. The screen showed there were text messages waiting.

'Least we know he won't be calling anyone,' Billy muttered to himself. He hesitated a moment before looking in the rear-view mirror; Darren was still walking up the driveway. A small smile spread across Billy's mouth and, he twisted the key in the ignition. The engine fired up and, the idea continuing to grow in his mind, Billy selected reverse. He tapped the horn and as per his plan, Darren turned to see what the problem was. Billy twisted round in his seat and gestured through the rear window for Darren to come back.

Darren muttered something unheard and started back towards the car. Billy released the handbrake.

Kevin froze on the other side of the thicket he'd pushed through. He heard the car's engine, he heard the horn. He even heard the quick, panicked yell from Darren before the sound of the car hitting him was heard. Quickly, he about turned and pushed back through the thicket, scratching his skin up on the thorns in the process. He made it back to the driveway in time to see the car drive back over Darren's body; the wheel crushed his head as though it were nothing but a soft watermelon.

'What the fuck are you doing?'

Billy pulled the car to a standstill. His eyes fixed on Kevin. Slowly, Billy smiled and gave him a little wave.

Kevin asked again, 'What are you doing?'

When Billy had seen the phone, it had dawned on him that he didn't have any footage on his own device showing *his* face. Every clip he had filmed showed the others though, clearly.

He knew the likelihood of finding Adam was slim to none given the fact they were in the middle of nowhere so - best he could do was clean house.

The way Billy saw it, Adam would need to remember what they all looked like in order for a search to be put out and Billy had purposely not looked at him too often, opting to look out of the window instead, whilst they were driving.

Darren and Kevin though?

They'd both stared him right out so, chances were, Adam would be able to give a good description of *them* more than *him*. Worse? Billy knew that, if Kevin or Darren *were* caught, they would quickly give him up in order to get themselves a reduced sentence. It was the kind of people they were.

Billy slipped the car into first and slammed his foot down on the accelerator.

Like an idiot, Kevin stood there a moment as he tried to comprehend what the hell was going on. When his brain finally kicked in, it was too late.

24

Tessa waited outside the door of the spare bedroom for a moment then pushed it open and walked in, closing it once more behind her.

She slapped on the lights, the single, unshaded bulb hanging from the ceiling casting a dull glow over the room and its contents.

Tessa glanced around, thinking she really should tidy up in here. Get rid of some of the empty boxes, make some more room for herself. But it would wait for now. She had more pressing matters to deal with.

Chris Whiteman was lying in one corner of the room although a quick glance could have mistaken his hunched body for a pile of blood stained rags. His head was slumped onto his chest, his knees drawn up so that he was in a foetal position.

His wrists and his ankles were both secured firmly by the zip-ties that Tessa had used to manacle him. A grey cloth had been stuffed into his mouth, held in place by a piece of rope. As Tessa moved closer to him she could

see that his eyes were closed. He seemed to be unconscious but she kept her distance, wondering if he was
feigning it.

The kitchen knife that she'd jammed into him moved
up and down gently with each breath he took.

Tessa looked more closely at it thinking that she
couldn't have damaged anything vital when she stuck it
in him because he was still alive. If she'd cut through
his intestines or ruptured an organ like the liver or
spleen then surely the injury would have killed him.

Wouldn't it?

Sure enough, the blade was in the meaty part of his
torso, below the rib cage and above the hip and she
guessed that an inch or two of the steel had penetrated
him.

He had lost quite a bit of blood though. The crimson
fluid was still seeping from the wound now but Tessa
realised that the metal was actually working like a cork.
The really heavy bleeding wouldn't occur until it was
removed. How much of that bleeding was happening
internally now she had no idea and, if she was honest,
she didn't really care.

She took a step closer to him and prodded one of his legs with her foot.

Chris Whiteman didn't move.

Tessa tried again, this time kicking him harder.

Whiteman sighed and shifted position slightly.

Tessa kicked him again.

He opened his eyes slightly, blinked a few times then closed them again.

'I know you can hear me,' she said, quietly. She leaned forward and tugged the cloth from his mouth.

Whiteman tried to take a deep breath but the pain seemed to dissuade him. He coughed, bright blood flecking his lips and chin.

'I need a doctor,' he croaked.

'You should have thought of that before you tried to rape me,' Tessa snapped.

'I didn't rape you,' Whiteman groaned.

'You would have done.'

'Listen, just get me a doctor will you? I'm in a lot of pain.'

'So I'm supposed to care about your pain am I? Did you think about my feelings when you burst in here and tried to rape me? No you didn't.'

'Just get me a fucking doctor,' Whiteman snarled through clenched teeth.

'You don't give the orders. Not now,' she told him, flatly. 'I'm in charge now.'

Whiteman winced and coughed again.

Tessa sat down on the floor a couple of feet away from him, drawing her feet up beneath her.

'So what are you going to do?' Whiteman asked. 'Sit there and watch me die?'

'I can think of worse things to do. And you'd deserve it.'

His demeanour suddenly changed. His face, already pale, took on an expression of pleading.

'Please get me a doctor,' he gasped. 'I'm in a lot of pain.'

'Ask me nicely,' Tessa said, smiling thinly.

'What?'

'You want a doctor? Ask nicely. You wanted me to suck your cock didn't you? You wanted me to ask. You wanted me to say what you wanted to hear. Well now you can say what I want to hear. You can beg me. The way you wanted me to say those horrible things you were going to make me say.'

'You're fucking sick,' Whiteman hissed.

'But *I'm* not dying,' Tessa said.

They regarded each other evenly for a moment then Tessa leaned forward slightly.

'Did you get them all to say those disgusting things before you raped them?' she wanted to know.

'What the fuck are you talking about?' he grunted.

'The other women you raped. There must have been others. You seemed very...accomplished when it came to trying to frighten me. You've obviously done it before.'

He shook his head.

'I don't know what you're talking about,' Whiteman said, lowering his gaze.

'Yes you do,' she chided. 'Come on, tell me. How many others have you raped?'

'Fuck off.'

'That's no way to talk to the person who can decide whether you live or die is it?'

He coughed, more blood spilling over his lips.

'Can't you take these off?' he asked, holding up his arms to show her how the zip-ties had cut into the flesh of his wrists.

'So you can rape me? Do you think I'm stupid?' Tessa snapped.

'I'm not going to rape you in this condition am I?' Whiteman countered.

'You're not going to rape anyone again if I have anything to do with it,' Tessa told him.

'Just let me go,' he groaned. 'Let me get out of here.'

'So you can do it to some other girl? So you can come back here and attack *me* again?'

'Just let me out and you'll never see me again, I promise.'

'Like I'm going to believe a promise made by you?' Tessa chuckled. The sound had a mocking tone that Whiteman wasn't slow to pick up.

He strained against the bonds, lunging forward slightly.

'Fucking let me go,' he snarled.

Tessa slowly got to her feet.

'Where are you going?' he wanted to know.

'I've got things to do,' she told him, quietly, moving nearer and picking up the cloth she'd stuffed into his mouth earlier. 'More important things than sitting in here listening to your lies.'

She tossed the cloth at him.

'You can scream and shout all you want to,' she went on. 'I've already told the neighbours my new TV has a really loud volume. No one will care if they hear you. But if you do make a noise, I'll come back in here and I'll cut one of your ears off.'

'You wouldn't fucking dare,' Whiteman said but there was no conviction in his voice.

'You want to try me?' Tessa said.

Then she turned and left the room.

As she reached the sitting room the phone rang.

25

Tessa froze.

She had a land line, mainly to allow her to have inter-net but she could count the calls she'd had on it on one hand during the three years she'd lived in the flat.

Who the hell was calling her?

And at a time like this? Who was calling at the height of a world wide medical emergency?

She moved towards the phone, the strident tone still reverberating around the flat.

All her friends called her on her mobile. No one used the land line.

She stood looking down at the phone, reaching out tentatively for the receiver.

Just pick the fucking thing up.

She finally grabbed the receiver and lifted it to her ear.

'Hello,' she said, softly.

'Hello, is that Tessa Meyer,' said the unbearably up-beat voice at the other end of the line.

Tessa frowned.

'Yes,' she said, falteringly.

'Hello, my name is Leon and I'm calling from Deep Clean,' said the voice.

Tessa moved the phone away from her ear slightly, taken aback not only by the call but also by the tone of the callers voice. She wondered for a moment if he was on some kind of drug.

'The reason for the call is that we here at Deep Clean have a cleaning process for eliminating Corona Virus and SARS and...'

'Wait a minute, are you cold calling me?' Tessa said, a slight smile forming on her lips.

'I'm calling to tell you about this new deep cleaning process we have,' Leon continued, determined to get through his script irrespective of the reaction at the other end of the line. 'It kills 99.9% of all viruses, including Corona and SARS.'

'You are kidding, right?' Tessa said.

'Here at Deep Clean we've got new technology that can kill viruses like Corona Virus and SARS.'

'So a call centre has found the cure for Corona Virus?' Tessa offered, smiling broadly.

'I can get my manager to call you, to give you more details,' Leon persisted.

'Where did you get my number?' Tessa wanted to know.

'From a database.'

'Really?'

'We're allowed to do that.'

'I'm surprised you had time in between finding the cure for Corona Virus.'

'It isn't a cure,' Leon admitted. 'It's what our deep cleaning does. It kills every virus there is, including Corona virus.'

'So, the greatest scientific brains in the world haven't found a cure but you guys have?'

There was a momentary silence at the end of the line. Then, it seemed Leon found the place in his script where he'd been before Tessa broke his train of thought.

'This is the most comprehensive deep clean you've ever seen,' Leon went on.

'I'm sure it is,' Tessa giggled.

'I can get my manager to call you,' Leon continued.

'How much would this cost me then?'

'The call is absolutely free. It's just in case you have any questions to ask him about the process.'

'Well, the main question I have is why you're cold calling people like this when all everyone else is bothered about is not getting ill or dying? It's a bit obscene to be honest.'

Another silence.

'Have you been calling other people?' Tessa wanted to know.

'Oh, yes,' Leon trilled as if what he'd just said was worthy of applause.

'Mostly old people?'

'Well, mostly but we ring anyone.'

'You should be ashamed,' Tessa said, quietly.

She heard Leon take a deep breath at the other end of the line.

'So, when would you like me to book you in for a call?' he offered at last.

Tessa shook her head.

'I don't want a call thank you and I'd like it if you didn't call here again. Thank you.'

She put the phone down feeling a little angry that Leon had called her. It was incredible that some people were trying to make money out of the Corona Virus while the rest of the world was in such a state of fear and dread. It seemed that the worldwide pandemic inspired not just horror but also the entrepreneurial spirit. She looked down at the phone once again as if waiting for it to burst into life again but, needless to say, it didn't.

She wandered across to the kitchen area where she first put on the kettle and then went to a drawer.

Tessa opened it and looked down at the contents.

She selected two large kitchen knives, one of them about twelve inches longer and serrated.

The straight bladed one she inspected closely, pressing her thumb gently against the sharpened edge. It was viciously sharp and she hissed as she opened a hairline cut on the pad of the digit. She stuck the thumb in her mouth, sucking gently, inspecting the cut after a moment or two. It had stopped bleeding but it stung a little. Tessa made a mental note not to do anything so stupid again.

However, she was happy with how sharp the knife was.

It would do perfectly.

26.

It did the job.

Billy sat up in the seat. His nose was split across the bridge from where he had head butted the steering wheel. His head pounded and he couldn't help but feel stupid. He could have had the desired results using half the speed he'd slammed into Kevin with but... *He fucked up.*

Kevin was pinned between the front of Adam's car and the tree Billy had managed to hit, having ploughed through the thicket. He was alive with a trickle of dark red blood coming from the corner of his mouth which suggested some internal damage within his battered body. He probably wouldn't be alive for much longer.

Billy opened the car door and pushed himself from the driver's seat. He slumped to the ground, landing hard on his side with an *oof* forced from his throat. He laid there a moment with the world around him spinning.

'W…W….' Kevin swallowed a mouthful of claret and tried again. 'W…Why?'

Billy took a lungful of air in, grabbing what was needed. Slowly he let it out as he said, 'It was you or me.'

It had only taken Billy a matter of minutes to decide that Adam would have reported his friends but not him. Seconds after that, Billy had deduced that it would be his friends who'd be the ones to turn him in. Less time after that? They were dead or dying and whilst he might be hurting - at least he would stay free.

Kevin scrambled for the words, 'B…But….I… Didn't…D…D….Do…. Any……Thing….'

Billy slowly got up from the dirt. He leaned down on the bonnet of the car and continued to catch his breath.

He said to Kevin, 'But you would have… The police would have come knocking and you would have done anything you could to save yourself. Same with that cunt,' he pointed back to Darren's body. 'Everyone in this world… You're all just out for yourselves, same as me.' He continued, 'Look at the world and it's the same for every cunt in it now. People breaking the social distancing rules, looking to scam others out of money, being selfish by stock-piling their food and fucking toilet rolls, spreading their fucking germs around because they think they're fucking invincible. It's in our nature to be selfish and...' He shrugged. 'It's in our nature to look out for ourselves... I've done fuck all different to what a normal person would do.' He paused a moment before he asked, 'Do you know what they call it?'

Kevin's eyes were fixed. His pained breathing now silent. He'd heard nothing of what Billy had said. Regardless, Billy finished.

'They call it survival of the fittest.'

Billy stood there a moment, looking at his dead friend and the state of the car. Like his friends, the car was fucked too but, no loss. A quick wipe down of his prints and he could just walk back to town. It would take a while but, now it was less about social distancing and more about *crime-distancing*. "This" crime at least.

Billy patted his dead friend on the shoulder and said, 'Survival of the fittest, my friend, and I am fitter than all of you...'

He laughed.

'Fitter than anyone who dares stand in my way…'

He coughed before growling to clear his throat. Damn thing had been sore for a few days now.

*

Sophie Hall looked at the coughing idiot with disdain in her eyes. All day at work she had had to be dealing with such people, telling them (politely) to step behind the yellow line at her till point. The all important 2 metre rule. Now though, outside her closed store and wearing a jacket over her uniform, she didn't need to be polite.

'Can you get the fuck back? Seriously!'

Sophie was standing at the bus stop. Most of the other people standing there were abiding by the *distancing* rule, except this fucking twat.

Great, she thought, *sent home from work early after they shut the store down due to a stabbing in the car park, only to get infected with corona virus at the bus-stop.*

The man looked at her like she was a piece of shit. Like so many people in the country, he had grown tired of being told what to do. 'Wind your fucking neck in,' he said with venom dripping from his tone. 'You want to stand further away from me? You're welcome to fucking move.'

Sophie shook her head. Of course no one else got involved either. They all just stood, looking down at the concrete.

'Need a lift?' A familiar voice distracted Sophie from responding to the stranger. It was Steve Matthewman, sitting in his car that he'd pulled up close to the bus stop. He too had been sent home after the closure of the store.

Sophie smiled when she saw him.

'I'm heading in that direction anyway,' he continued.

'So long as you're sure?'

'Of course.'

Steve leaned across to the passenger seat and wiped it clean of the few chocolate wrappers he'd left there. Then, he opened the door for her.

Sophie climbed in and closed the door behind her.

'You're a life-saver,' she said. 'I thought I was about to have to kill someone.'

'Oh?'

'Idiot was standing close to me and coughing. Even with all the news bulletins, the headlines on the front of papers, signs in stores... He still can't keep his distance from me *and* he had a cough. Disgusting.'

'That's the human-race for you.'

Steve pulled away and as he joined the road, they passed the bus headed for the waiting passengers.

27

When Tessa walked back into the spare bedroom she was carrying a mug of tea with her.

She pushed open the door and looked in, trying to see in the gloom if Whiteman was asleep, unconscious or awake. She couldn't tell if his eyes were open from her vantage point at the door so she walked further into the room, switching on the light as she did.

As she got closer to Whiteman he stirred and turned to face her.

'I brought you a cup of tea,' she told him.

He eyed her suspiciously.

'I can't hold the fucking cup,' he snapped, holding up his bound hands.

'I brought you a straw,' she told him, pulling one from the back pocket of her jeans.

She crouched down near him, slipped the straw into the mug and pushed it towards him.

'You think of everything don't you?' he chided.

'I like to be prepared.'

He sipped some of the tea and then sat back again.

'I need to have a piss,' he said, his face pale.

'Go on then,' she said.

'I need the toilet,' Whiteman snapped.

'If you need to go, you can do it there, I'm not letting you out of this room.'

'You're one sick fucking bitch,' he snorted.

'I think you called me that before and, like I said, that's pretty rich coming from a rapist.'

'Oh shut up. I didn't rape you. But you might have *killed* me. You'll be a murderer if I die. If you don't get me a doctor.'

'So you think I'm going to call you an ambulance do you?'

'You stabbed me,' Whiteman shouted.

Tessa held his gaze, keeping the mug of tea at arm's length.

'Are you going to drink some more of this or not?' she asked.

Whiteman leaned forward slightly and fastened his lips around the end of the straw again.

He took a sip, gulping it down thirstily. She kept the mug there as he continued to swallow as much as he could.

'If I let you out of this room you'll try to escape,' she went on, withdrawing the mug slightly.

Whiteman glared silently at her.

'Can I have some more?' he asked, opening his mouth.

'You forgot the magic word,' Tessa told him.

'Can I have some more, *cunt*,' he sneered.

She smiled and shook her head.

'You don't learn do you?' she told him. 'Do you speak to everyone like this?'

'No, just to people who fucking stab me and tie me up in a room.'

'Have you got any family?' Tessa wanted to know.

'That's none of your business,' he sneered.

'I just wondered if you had a sister. You must have a mother. Do you speak to her like that? Do you hate all women? Was it something your mother did to you when you were little? Is that why you hate women?'

'I don't hate women,' he said.

'You must have a problem with them if you can burst in here like you did and do the things you do. Rapists are all about the power, not the sex. What made you the way you are?'

'Did you tie me up in here so you could analyse me?'

'I don't really care about you. What made you the way you are. Why you're such a vile specimen but now it's in my power to make sure you don't do it again.'

'Just give me some more fucking tea,' Whiteman hissed.

'You want it, have it.' She threw the tea at him, most of it hitting him in the face. 'You've drunk enough anyway. What I put in it will start to take effect soon.'

'What are you talking about?' he hissed.

'I put 20 mg of Haloperidol in your tea. They use it in Intensive Care to keep people sedated. The usual dose is 2.5mg but I wanted to be sure it worked on you.'

Whiteman clenched his jaws together.

'It causes diminished motor activity,' she went on. 'I learned about it from my sister, she used to be a nurse in an intensive care unit. I visited her there one day, that was when I stole it.'

Whiteman moved back slightly, his gaze still fixed on Tessa.

'You *are* fucking crazy,' he said, softly.

'No, no, no. I was just protecting myself. I'm not very strong you see. I needed a little...chemical help.' She chuckled and the sound made him shiver. 'I've used it on the others too. It always worked.'

'Others?' Whiteman murmured.

'Do you think you're the first?' she told him. 'You're all the same. You think you can barge in here and do whatever you like. You think you can treat me or any other woman like some animal.' Tessa shook her head.

'Just let me go now and I won't tell the police,' Whiteman said.

Again Tessa chuckled.

She got to her feet and walked across the room towards a pile of cardboard boxes. As Whiteman watched she began to remove them, finally revealing what looked like a large chest freezer behind them. She lifted the lid and reached inside, taking something out.

When Whiteman saw what she was holding he screamed.

28

Adam screamed with joy when he saw the house. Without hesitating, he pushed through the brambles, snagging his clothes in the process. He knew it would hurt going through the thicket but he didn't care; not when he had seen the old farmhouse on the other side of it. His only thought now was to get to the building, ask to use their phone and wait for help to get there.

As he pushed through the last of the brambles, he fell to the long grass leading the way up to the back of the house.

There was a temptation to call out for help but he resisted. He didn't think *they* would be able to track him to here but, in case they were looking for him and close, it made sense to be as quiet as he could. Just get to the house, knock on the door and hope to God someone is home.

Of course they would be home, there's a quarantine in place... The voice in his head reminded him, *Oh, you mean the quarantine most people are ignoring?*

Adam staggered up to his feet and then started running towards the house. The sweat ran down his forehead and back; a lack of looking after his health over the years showed via dark patches of sweat beneath his shirt.

To Adam's relief, he noticed one of the doors open and an older guy appear in the doorway.

'Not again!' The man, John Burley, shouted as he waved Adam away with an open-handed gesture, 'Why can't you leave us alone?'

From the distance, Adam could barely make out what John was saying. He called out, 'I need your help! Please!' Just as Adam struggled to hear his words, so did John struggle to hear his.

As Adam continued running towards the building, the old man disappeared inside for a moment before he stepped back into sight with a shotgun in hand. When he raised it up, Adam immediately froze with his hands in the air.

'Wait! Wait! I just need your help!'

John stepped from his property and started stalking towards Adam with the gun raised up, ready to fire. To further show he wasn't a threat, Adam dropped to his knees.

'I just need help,' Adam said loudly.

*

BEFORE

This was the part of the job Joanne Ormshaw hated; letting friends and relatives know that, despite the doctors' best efforts, they hadn't been able to save a loved one. She took a deep breath and held it for a second before she opened the door to the relatives' waiting room.

'Mr. Burley?'

John stood up the moment she said his name. 'Yes. How is she?'

In truth, he didn't need to ask the question. The grim news needing to be delivered was written all over Joanne's face.

'I'm terribly sorry but…'

The rest of her words merged to nothing but white noise as John's world collapsed around him. The love of his life, his darling wife... They'd thought it had just been a cold to start with but then the symptoms got more severe. Her limbs ached and her chest hurt as she struggled to breathe. Before they had time to take stock of what was happening; she was on a ventilator and he wasn't permitted in to see her. Now this.

'She survived cancer just for this to happen,' John said as Joanne's words started to make sense to him once more as she asked if he was okay.

'I'm terribly sorry, we did everything that we possibly could but...'

'How is it fair? What did she do to deserve the cancer, let alone this? She was a good person. She had a big heart... And...' his words trailed off.

'I really am sorry.' She asked, 'Is there someone you would like us to call?'

John shook his head. 'There was only us,' he said quietly.

*

NOW

'What? You didn't take enough the first time?' John was practically shouting. The veins on the side of his neck were bulging as his stress levels shot through the roof. He was just a few feet away from where Adam was kneeling with his hands raised in the air defensively.

'Please... I don't know who you think I am but, you're mistaken. I don't know you! I don't *fucking* know you! I'm in trouble and I was just hoping to borrow a phone and...'

'You think I was born yesterday? You don't think I know all your tricks?' He still came closer with the barrels of the shotgun aimed directly at Adam's head. 'You know I lost my wife that day? The day you and your friends decided to swing on by?'

'I swear... I don't know what the fuck you are talking about! I just wanted to use your...'

'Shut up!'

Adam stopped talking.

'My wife was dead and then you dirty bastards thought you would come by and take everything else I owned...'

*

BEFORE

John stood in the doorway of his home with a look of shock on his face and his mouth agape. All around, his drawers had been emptied and his furniture turned upside down. Tall cupboards, once filled with fine china, had been toppled with the contents smashed across the floor in tiny, sharp fragments.

John's eyes scanned the damage done and noted a steaming turd in the middle of the hallway; another fuck you from whoever had broken in and done this.

The country was meant to be in lock down and for the most part they were. But of course the bad element wouldn't listen. Even on the night the Prime Minister announced the lockdown, some people were out setting fire to ambulances and burning buildings down.

John shook his head.

Of course they'd be breaking into places too. All he could think was, it was a good job he had been out...

But if they came back... He had something special for them locked away in a metal cabinet upstairs.

Just let them try it.

*

NOW

'You think I would just stand by and let you do it to me again?'

'I swear I have no idea what you're talking about! I was in the house further down the road... I was forced to drive these...'

The gunshot rung through the air as Adam's head exploded. His headless body slumped to the dirt. John just stood there a moment, emotionless. Exhausted. Smoke billowed from one of the gun's two barrels.

John sighed.

The world had changed. People had changed. And, chances were, they would never go back to how they once were.

Whether that was a good thing, or a bad thing, re-mained to be seen…

John turned the gun on himself. One more barrel to let off.

'No one nice left in the damned world,' he muttered.

His finger touched upon the trigger.

29.

Whiteman had no idea how long the severed human head that Tessa had lifted from the freezer had been in there.

It had belonged to someone roughly the same age as him as far as he could see although he found it difficult to concentrate on the details.

The eyes were closed, at least one of them was. The left eyelid was propped partially open by the thick white material on it that resembled frost on open ground. There was more of it along the eyebrows and around the lips.

As Tessa moved closer with the hideous trophy, Whiteman could see that there was more of it on the stump of the neck.

Tessa held the head a foot or so from him, allowing him to take in every detail.

As she looked down she saw a dark stain spreading across his groin and the top of his thighs.

'You fucking crazy bitch,' Whiteman whimpered, trying to push himself away from Tessa who merely stood there motionless, the head still gripped in her fist, secured by the hold she had on its hair. Droplets of melting ice actually fell from the stump of the neck, some of them dripping onto Whiteman.

He was shaking uncontrollably by now, watching as Tessa turned back to the chest freezer and dropped the head unceremoniously back into it. As he watched she reached in and pulled something else out.

As she brandished it before her he could see that it was a human arm.

Severed at the shoulder and wrist, it extended stiffly in Tessa's grip.

'Who the fuck did that belong to?' Whiteman gasped.

'Does it matter?' Tessa muttered. "I can't remember his name anyway.'

'Why?" he gaped.

'I told you why. He tried to hurt me. He deserved it. Just like you.'

She turned back and looked at Whiteman who was now struggling to keep his eyes open, his body sagging forward.

'The Haloperidol is taking effect,' she mused. 'Another five minutes and you'll be under.'

'What the fuck are you talking about?' Whiteman sobbed.

'It'll numb your muscles,' Tessa told him. 'You won't feel...much. You'll still be awake but...'

Whiteman gasped loudly, sliding a little further down until he was lying flat on the floor.

'You won't get away with this,' he whimpered.

'Why not? I got away with the other three,' Tessa told him, flatly.

'You've murdered three people?' Whiteman gasped.

'I don't look at it as murder. I look at it as justice.'

Whiteman was struggling to keep his eyes open now. He could barely raise his head and look at her as she began to pull off his trainers. She tossed them aside and pulled off his socks before moving up his body to his waist.

There she began undoing his jeans, finally tugging them free.

She used a small knife to cut away the material of his t-shirt and hoodie that was adjacent to the blade of the kitchen knife she'd stuck in him what seemed like an age ago.

She pulled the blood soaked garments free and threw those aside too.

Whiteman was now naked but for his boxers and Tessa looked down contemptuously at him.

'Please,' he said and it sounded as if he was drunk. He could barely move his lips now. They felt numb when he tried to move them. Just like the rest of his body. Spittle dribbled from one corner of his mouth.

Tessa smiled down at him and used the small knife to cut away the material of his boxers, dragging them free so that he now lay completely naked before her.

She held the small knife tightly and slid the tip across his testicles, stirring some of the hairs there.

If Whiteman had been able to protest he would have, but all he could do was lay immobile as Tessa then took the tip of the blade and trailed it from his testicles, slowly up his shaft to the bulbous head of his penis.

She looked at him, holding his terrified gaze for a second then she carefully pushed the tip of the blade into his urethra. A matter of millimeters. She held it there for what seemed like an eternity and then withdrew it, thinking how easy it would be to slice his penis in two with the knife.

'I'm not going to do that,' she told him. 'I'm not going to hurt you any more than I have to. I'm not like that. I wouldn't cause you pain the way you were going to cause me pain.'

She got slowly to her feet and headed for the door, watched by Whiteman who could now barely move his eyes in their sockets due to muscular paralysis. He did see her return though and he knew that she was now carrying an even larger knife. It was fully a foot long and it gleamed ominously in the dull light.

She walked back across to him and hunkered down beside his chest, looking at him as if she was taking in every inch of his body.

Or deciding where to cut first.

'My dad was a butcher,' she told him. 'He taught me everything he knew.' She smiled broadly. 'There's not much difference butchering a human body then there is when preparing a cow or a pig carcass.' She gently pressed the point of the large knife against his chest. 'It's just that the animals are dead by the time they get to the butcher.' Her smile broadened.

Whiteman's eyes widened a little more.

'There isn't so much of a human body that's edible when you compare it to a sheep or a pig though,' she went on. 'There's hardly a part of the pig that doesn't get eaten. Right down to the ears and the trotters. Some people even eat the brains you know but I wouldn't want to do that with a human.' She wrinkled her face. 'Yuk.' Again she smiled.

She prodded his thigh with the knife.

'The most meat is here,' she said. 'On the legs. On the buttocks. Even if someone is fat it doesn't mean that their belly is going to make good eating. Just because there's more of it. And you have to be so careful about how you cook it.'

Whiteman was beginning to wish he *was* dead.

'The internal organs are best,' Tessa continued happily. 'The liver, the kidneys, even the lung can be cooked if it's done properly.'

Whiteman made a low gurgling sound in his throat. A last exhalation of despair?

'People think that the virus can live on the surface of the skin,' Tessa told him. 'But no one knows enough about this Corona Virus to know if it can penetrate into the muscles and, even if it does, if the flesh is cooked for long enough then the virus will die. Any virus will die if the temperature is high enough and constant enough. They keep telling us that on the news.' She smiled down at him, bringing the knife against his throat. 'They tell us so much on the news, don't they? About how we should all stay in. How we should keep away from other people. How we should care for others.' The smile slipped from her face. 'Perhaps you should have thought about that.'

She dragged the knife across his throat with incredible strength.

The cut severed his windpipe and both his carotid arteries and sliced down almost as far as his spine.

A huge gout of blood erupted from the gaping gash, some of it spattering Tessa who seemed oblivious to the crimson cascade.

She cut again.

And again.

30

Claire Bennett heard the knocking on the door and turned to look at Peter Miller.

'Did you hear that?' she said, quietly. 'I thought I heard knocking.'

Peter glanced up from his book and cocked an ear in the direction of the sound.

He merely shook his head.

'I heard someone knocking,' Claire insisted.

'Go and check,' he offered, turning the page of the huge volume of Napoleonic history he was reading.

'Are you ever going to finish that?' Claire said, smiling, tapping the cover of the book as she passed him. 'You've been reading it for ages.'

'It's over seven hundred pages,' he reminded her, holding up the massive tome. 'I'm not a bloody speed reader you know.'

Claire chuckled and made her way out of the room, heading for the door. As she drew closer to it she heard another knock.

Peering through the spy-hole she saw that Tessa was standing outside.

Claire slipped the chain and opened the door.

'Hey, you,' she said, smiling. 'Are you okay?'

'I don't know if you saw the latest news bulletin,' Tessa announced.

'No. We're trying to avoid the bloody news channels,' Claire confessed. 'It's too depressing.'

'Well, starting tomorrow, they're closing the smaller supermarkets because people are still panic buying.'

'People are such fucking dickheads,' Claire sighed. 'What the hell are we supposed to do for food?'

'They're going to introduce a rationing system they say but not for food, for people's time. They're going to stop everyone going out and just have designated food buyers who'll deliver to houses.'

'How the hell can they do that?'

'The buyers will all have been tested negative for Corona. No one who hasn't been tested is going to be allowed out.'

'Oh Jesus,' Claire sighed, slumping against the door frame. 'This is getting worse isn't it?'

'I don't think enough people did as they were told when it first started. It's like fifty per cent of the population did and fifty per cent didn't. And now we're all going to suffer for it.'

Peter appeared behind Claire and smiled broadly at Tessa.

'Hello again,' he chuckled, watching as Tessa brought her hand out from behind her back and produced a substantial looking package wrapped in silver foil.

'I thought you two might like this,' Tessa announced. 'I cooked some earlier but there's far too much for just me.'

She passed the package to Claire who pulled back the foil slightly.

'What is it?' she asked.

'It's like a meat substitute,' Tessa told them. 'I bought loads of it when I was in my vegan stage a year or so ago.' She laughed. 'It tastes okay though, especially if you put plenty of gravy or seasoning on it.'

'That's very kind of you, Tessa,' Peter said. 'Are you sure you want to give it away? You could freeze it. Keep it for ages to tide you over.'

'No, it's fine. I've got loads of it, honestly. I thought you might like it. Especially with these new measures coming in.'

Claire leaned forward and kissed Tessa lightly on the cheek.

'Social distancing,' Peter said, trying to look stern.

'You're so kind,' Claire said to Tessa, beaming. 'We'll have some of this tonight for dinner. I hate cooking anyway.'

'Yes, it shows,' Peter said, smiling.

'Cheeky bastard,' Claire grunted, slapping his arm.

They all laughed and Claire momentarily disappeared, taking the foil wrapped package into the kitchen before returning a moment later.

'Closing supermarkets?' she murmured as she returned.

'They said just the smaller ones to start with but, if things don't improve then they'll clamp down and start using the food buyers so people actually do stay indoors,' Tessa sighed.

'What more can they do?' Peter mused.

'They said that the police were going to start enforcing restrictions even more stringently,"'Tessa went on. 'The fines for public gatherings are going up. Anyone found outside without a passport and I.D can be arrested on the spot.'

'Fuck,' Peter sighed.

'At least they haven't made *that* against the law yet,' Claire giggled.

'Good job they haven't,' Tessa chuckled. 'Or you two would be locked up. Peter told me about your little adventure this morning.'

All three of them laughed. It was a pleasing sound, filling the stairwell and the area around the entrance to Peter and Claire's flat. A sound that hadn't been heard for far too long inside the little block.

'I would ask you in to have some dinner with us,' Claire said. 'But, with this social distancing and that...' She let the sentence trail off.

'I know, besides, my dinner is on downstairs. It'll be ready soon but thanks anyway,' Tessa replied. 'Maybe when all of this is over we could get together.'

'That's a date,' Peter grinned.

'Definitely,' echoed Claire.

'If I find any more of that meat substitute I don't want I'll bring it up,' Tessa said, turning and heading back towards the stairs.

'Thanks, Tessa,' Claire called.

'You're welcome,' Tessa said. 'Enjoy.'

She headed back down the steps, her footsteps echoing inside the stairwell. They stood there until they heard her door close behind her then both turned back into their own flat.

'That's really kind of her isn't it?' Claire said, walking into the kitchen. She peeled back the silver foil and looked more closely at the contents. 'This will last us for a few days by the look of it. I'll do some vegetables with it. It should be lovely.'

'She's a nice girl,' Peter called.

'You just fancy her,' Claire chuckled.

'Maybe a little bit,' Peter confessed, walking up behind Claire and snaking his arms around her waist.

She pushed her buttocks back against him and sighed as he kissed her neck.

'Do you want dinner right now?' she purred.

'No,' he said, smiling. 'It can wait for an hour or so.'
They both laughed.

31

The rain that had been threatening to fall all day finally arrived with the onset of darkness.

Tessa sat at her window peering out into the growing gloom, watching as rain drops ran down the glass.

She always seemed to feel the isolation more when night came. It was as if the disappearance of the light and the sunshine just added to her mordant state of mind. The earlier news that her infrequent short trips out of the flat for food were to be curtailed had certainly not helped her mood. She wondered just how much worse this situation could get. People were still dying. There didn't seem to be a marked slowing down in the numbers catching Corona virus. The death toll was still rising. There was still no sign of a cure or even of more widespread testing for the insidious killer.

Tessa shuddered involuntarily.

She picked at her dinner, prodding it with a fork every now and then as she shifted position on her chair close to the window.

From her vantage point she could see the road and pathway before her and she saw a car pull up in front of the flats across the road.

A figure clambered from it and scampered across the tarmac towards the building. They gave the car a wave goodbye as it drove off.

Tessa moved closer to the glass.

She recognised the woman who had got out of the car.

It was the woman from the supermarket wasn't it? Sophie (according to her badge).

Tessa smiled, surprised at her own powers of observation and also her own recall.

I didn't know she lived around here. But then again why would you? The sense of community and the interest in those living nearby only seemed to have come about in the middle of this global pandemic.

Tessa watched as the woman disappeared inside the building, the car that had dropped her pulling away. She turned slightly, glancing in the direction of the television set. As she did a fresh bulletin flashed up on the screen.

'Due to the continued bulk and panic buying that has been occurring at supermarkets, the government have

introduced more measures to combat this,' the news-reader announced. *'The police are to be given more powers to prevent this trend from continuing. They will now have the right to enter individual homes to inspect the amount of shopping that each householder has. If anyone is found to be hoarding a particular type of food, especially the more popular ones like pasta, dry rice, flour and eggs, the police have the authority to remove the excess.'*

Tessa frowned.

'These measures were announced at a press confer-ence earlier in the day by the Prime Minister who has now recovered from his own bout of Corona Virus infec-tion,' the newsreader went on. *'The police will be enter-ing houses and dwellings as of noon today to conduct what the Prime Minister called food searches. They have been prompted by the emergency services inability to obtain sometimes even the most rudimentary foods because of panic and bulk buying.'*

Tessa swallowed hard, her heart increasing its pace.

'Anyone refusing to comply with these measures will be arrested,' the newsreader continued. *'The Govern-*

ment feel that such Draconian measures are necessary to safeguard the health and well-being of the public.'

Tessa took a step backwards.

'The Police will be entitled to search all cupboards, fridges, deep freeze units and other food storage areas in every home.'

Tessa tried to swallow but her throat was suddenly dry.

Deep freeze.

She almost laughed. God help her if anyone looked inside the chest freezer in the second bedroom. She had to empty it as quickly as possible. Get everything out of it into a plastic bag then hide the bag somewhere. Anywhere. And she had to do it fast. She had to empty the freezer. Ensure that everything that had been hidden in there was taken out and disposed of. No matter how.

Tessa hurried out of the room towards the room, her heart thudding hard against her ribs. This wasn't happening.

Was it?

She had reached the door when she heard a loud banging on the flat door.

'Hello,' a voice on the other side of the partition called. 'This is the police. We're conducting a food search.'

Tessa froze.

The banging on the door came again. More insistent this time.

'Food search,' the voice called again. 'Can you let us in, please? This is the police.'

Tessa felt the colour drain from her face and she closed her eyes so tightly that white lights danced behind her eyelids.

'Miss Meyer,' the policeman called. 'Can you let us in, please?'

Tessa slumped against the wall.

The banging on the door continued.

For those of us living in these uncertain times, stay safe.

Made in the USA
Middletown, DE
23 October 2023

41306657R00123